The Other Side of the Door

Dark Stories

Tyler Miller

Nickle Bee Books
SPOKANE, WASHINGTON

Tyler Miller/Nickle Bee Books
16621 E Indiana Avenue C105
Spokane Valley, WA 99216
www.nicklebeebooks.com

Publisher's Note: This is a work of fiction. Names, characters,
places, and incidents are a product of the author's imagination.
Locales and public names are sometimes used for atmospheric
purposes. Any resemblance to actual people, living or dead, or
to businesses, companies, events, institutions, or locales is completely coincidental.

Book Layout & Design ©2013 - BookDesignTemplates.com
Book Cover Design by James, GoOnWrite.com

Ordering Information:
Additional print and ebooks are available for order online by
visiting NickleBeeBooks.com

The Other Side of the Door/Tyler Miller. -- 1st ed.
ISBN-10: 0692535144
ISBN-13: 978-0692535141

In Memory of Ronald E Miller

TABLE OF CONTENTS

Submitted for the approval of the Midnight Society...

Til Death Do Us

THE BOX ARRIVED Thursday morning without any kind of label. It was small and plain, and Kenny Perkins left it on the edge of his desk until just before noon. When he finally opened it—he heard a wispy scratching from inside the box as he did—he discovered his wife's severed finger and her wedding ring.

The severed finger lay shriveled like thin leather. Kenny could see the bone through the dull, translucent skin. The fingernail had grown long and jagged, its tip still that hideous shade of magenta Selma always wore. Now it looked more like blood. The final knuckle bent upward, pointing directly, accusingly, at Kenny.

Kenny set the box on the desk, stood and went to the door. He opened it softly.

"Yes, Mr. Perkins?"

"Julie, the box you brought in this morning, it didn't have any address on it. Did you notice who left it?"

His secretary shook her head. "It was at the door when I opened up. Is there a problem, Mr. Perkins?"

"None at all."

He shut the door.

It's not her's. It can't be. This is a sick joke, that's all.

He took a pen from his drawer and poked it into the box. A thick, roiling gurgle tumbled through his gut. The finger shifted. He saw the ring clearly. One large diamond in the center, four smaller rubies at the corners.

Selma's.

He'd proposed to Selma Nolan on July ninth of 1997. They were married that November. Eight years later, he killed her. He was careful. He planned every detail. Her body was never found. She had, as all the news reports pointed out, simply *vanished*. And no one had ever known the truth.

Kenny stared at the box. Stared at the ring.

Until now.

***

The next day the call came.

"Did I get your attention?"

Kenny knew immediately. "How did you—"

"Are you sure you want to talk about this over the phone?"

"Where do you want to meet?"

"There is a little diner on the west end of town. Edna's."

"I know it."

"Be there. Eight o'clock."

"How will I know you?"

"I will know you, Mr. Perkins."

And the man hung up.

***

He'd loved his wife. Thought she was The One. *Knew* it. For seven years they lived—he'd believed—happily. Later this blissful period seemed to Kenny hazy and surreal, like a fugue he'd stumbled through unable to awake.

Seven years that crashed to an end when their daughter was born.

Kenny steered the Escalade into the school parking lot. Kyra leaped up from the grass waving her arm and ran to the car.

"Hey, Daddy."

"Hey, pumpernickel."

Kyra thrust her Hello Kitty backpack onto the floorboard. Her bright red tennis shoes clumped atop the pack, kicking Hello Kitty squarely in the eye.

"I *hate* school," Kyra said.

"Uh-oh."

Selma's most beautiful feature—aside from her long, luxurious legs—had been her eyes. They were a rich, haunting blue, the color of evening sun atop the ocean. Kenny's own eyes were blue flecked with tiny shards of green and almond.

Kyra's eyes were a dull, muddy brown.

"Polly Poirer is a nasty twit," Kyra spat.

"I thought you two were friends."

"That was *last* year, Dad. We're not friends anymore."

"That's right."

Nobody saw anything. Nobody even suspected. Mr. Perkins is not a person of interest in this case. That's what they said. I was the grieving husband. Lost. Confused. Angry. It was perfect.

Perfect.

"Daddy, you're not even listening."

"Sorry, sweetheart. What were you saying?" He steered out of the lot, past the flaggers and onto the street.

"I was *saying* that Polly stole my journal and showed it to everyone. She showed it to Alan."

"I see."

"Alan *Millhouse*."

"And what did he think of your journal?"

Kyra folded her arms across her chest and huffed.

"You don't ask Alan *Millhouse* a question like *that*."

He'd noticed Kyra's eyes the day they brought her home. And he'd known. Two blue-eyed parents. One brown-eyed girl.

It broke his heart.

For almost a year he lived with the knowledge of Selma's betrayal. And in all that time she acted like she didn't *know*. That she didn't know that he knew. She thought he was a fool. That he was just going to let it stand.

But he wouldn't.

He didn't.

"You know," Kyra said. "Some days I just want to *kill* her."

***

There was only one customer in Edna's diner.

He wore a faded gray jacket pulled tight around narrow shoulders, the collar tipped up over his neck. A tangle of salt and pepper hair swept over his forehead above a ridiculous pair of black Raybans, the kind Bob Dylan used to wear indoors.

Kenny sat down quickly. He looked the man over. Didn't know him.

"Who are you?" he said.

"You killed your wife, Mr. Perkins."

Kenny's stole a glance at the waitress behind the counter.

"I told her you wouldn't be ordering anything."

"My wife disappeared. If you have information about where she went—"

"Bullshit," the man said. "You put her in a hole under the falls. You choked the life out of her and stuffed her in that hold and left her there to rot. "

"I don't know what you're talking about."

"Well then you won't mind at all if I have a talk with the local PD. Tell them I might know where they can find a certain missing woman. I hear the case is still open."

Kenny had considered this. But if the man wanted to turn Kenny over to the law, he'd have done so already. Whoever he was, the man wanted something else.

"You're not going to do that."

Raybans leaned back. "Don't try to outsmart me, Mr. Perkins. You think you're pretty clever, but you're not. I'll have that little chat with the PD, don't think I won't. If I see fit."

"Why don't you tell me what you want?"

"Fair enough." Raybans folded his hands on the table. "Murder, Mr. Perkins. Murder, plain and simple."

"I didn't murder my wife."

"You misunderstand me. I'm not talking about your wife."

"Then what..."

Kenny understood. He shook his head. "No."

"Yes, Mr. Perkins. You see."

"Absolutely not."

"You've done it once before. Maybe more than once."

"No, I haven't. I don't know what you're—"

Raybans slammed his hand down on the table. The salt shaker jolted, tipping over and spilling little white crystals across the counter. The waitress looked up from the coffee pot, waited, and then went back to changing filters.

"*Don't* tell me you didn't kill her," the man said, his teeth clenched. "I *know* what you did, *remember*? I dug up her body, *remember*? I cut her finger off her hand. You know what I used? Pruning shears. The one's my wife cuts roses with. Don't *fuck* with me, Mr. Perkins."

Kenny coughed into his hand, holding back a thin film of bile. He wanted something to drink. Something strong enough to burn out the sick in his throat.

"You want me to tell you more?"

Kenny shook his head.

"What do you want?"

"I told you."

"No. I won't do it."

"You *will*. Or I'll have that chat. And your daughter can spend the rest of her life visiting Daddy down in Walla Walla."

"There's no—"

"Evidence? You sure of that, Mr. Perkins?"

He'd *been* sure. For seven years. Totally, completely, unerringly sure.

"Who?" Kenny said at last.

"Shouldn't be a problem," Raybans said. "You already know her."

The man leaned forward.

They talked for some time.

***

Kyra held up the book.

"Not tonight, honey."

Her face drew down into a pout, her muddy brown eyes dour and weepy.

He loved her. She wasn't his—he knew that—but he loved her all the same.

"Just one chapter."

Kyra clapped her hands. Kenny sat beside her on the bed.

Kyra picked the books they read together every night. Currently, they were reading *The Strange Case of Doctor Jekyll and Mr. Hyde*, a choice Kenny found rather morbid for an eight-year-old girl. But her reading level was advanced, as her teachers often pointed out.

Teachers like Ms. Kingsley.

"Here, Daddy. Where I marked it. In Dr. Jekyll's letter, remember? He said he hadn't drank the potion for two months."

Kenny found the page. "*I began to be tortured with throes and longings, as of Hyde struggling for freedom: and at last, in an hour of moral weakness, I once again compounded and swallowed the transforming draught. My devil had been long caged, he came out roaring.*"

He stopped.

"Do you read this kind of stuff in school? Like in Ms. Kingsley's class?"

Kyra frowned. "Ms. Kingsley was last year, Daddy."

"I know, sweetheart. Did Ms. Kingsley read you books like this last year?"

"No. She only read...*nice* stories."

"You really liked Ms. Kingsley, didn't you?"

"She's my favorite. Ever and ever."

Kyra's new teacher, Mrs. Jenkins, was stern and frumpy and chilly as arctic night. Kyra didn't care much for Mrs. Jenkins.

"Does Ms. Kingsley have a husband?"

Kyra shook her head. "She doesn't go on dates. She said so." As if this were the only reasonable and proper way to be. "Read the story, Daddy."

He read.

When the story was over, Kenny kissed Kyra's head and pulled the blanket up to her chin.

"No nightmares, babycakes?"

"Nope."

In his own bed, he couldn't sleep. He thought of Kyra at Show and Tell. Parent Day. The Halloween Carnival. One image after another, and in all of them the sweet, smiling Ms. Kingsley flitted through like a morning dove, landing, perching, singing sweetly and bringing joy to all the little children. Kyra's favorite teacher. Ever and ever.

He couldn't do it.

What he needed, he thought as he drifted into fitful sleep, was a magic drought, like Doctor Jekyll. Something to release Mr. Hyde.

***

Kenny trudged five miles through the overgrown trail that wound from the back of the house through the woods to Guy Haines Falls. The last time he'd been here was seven years ago. With Selma.

Guy Haines Falls plummeted three hundred feet into a deep blue pool. Selma once said the sunlight glinted off the tumbling water and looked like diamonds. Kenny put the shovel on the ground and took off his boots.

He'd buried Selma in the hollow behind the falls.

He left his boots and shirt, but he took the shovel. He hissed when he stepped into the icy water. With long slow strokes he paddled to the end of the pool. Closing his eyes, he slipped under the falls and gripped the rocky ledge of the hollow.

He hoisted himself up.

At the back of the hollow was a narrow crevice in the rock. Seven years ago, he'd packed that crevice with dirt and rocks. Inside it lay Selma. What was left of her.

With the end of the shovel, Kenny stabbed at the thin membrane that closed the crevice. He bent and twisted. The rocks came loose. The mud slid free.

Like a gaping mouth, the crevice opened. Kenny knelt and peered inside.

Blackness.

He reached inside. A creeping prickle goosed his flesh.

She'll grab me and yank me in with her. To be with her forever.

But there was nothing there. Only rock and dirt and damp.

No. She has to be there. She can't be gone. She MUST BE—

She was gone.

Frantic, angry, he snatched up the shovel and flung it into the falls. He paced across the ledge. It wasn't possible. It wasn't fair. He tore at his hair. He kicked the rock wall. Finally, deflated, he sat on the ledge and cried.

When he swam back to the shore, the man was there.

"You're following me."

"Did you really think I'd leave her there?" Raybans said.

"Fuck you," Kenny spat.

He wished now he had the shovel, but it had sunk somewhere in the pond.

"She's been more...properly buried."

"You're sick. Sick and twisted."

"Says the pot to the kettle. There's only one way out of this."

"I'm not a murderer."

"I'm not sure your wife would agree. Or the police officers I'll be calling if you don't do what you're told."

"I'm not killing her. You can forget about it. Turn me in if you want. I won't do it."

"It's your choice, Mr. Perkins. It doesn't matter either way to me."

"The hell it doesn't."

Kenny waded out of the pool and reached for his boots.

"Either way, I get what I want. That's what you need to realize. This isn't about what you want, Mr. Perkins. It's what I want. And I get what I want. Guaranteed."

Kenny pulled on his boots. On the ground he spotted a thick, hand-sized rock. He stared.

"I see what you're thinking."

"Do you?"

"It's what I would be thinking too. And it's not a bad idea."

"Oh really."

"Except."

"Except what?"

Raybans drew his hand from his coat pocket. A snub nosed revolver dangled from his hand.

"Except."

Kenny looked away.

"You have a choice to make, Mr. Perkins. You've done it before, so it should be easier the second time around. Or you can choose jail. For the rest of your life."

"Who are you?" Kenny said.

"An angel of justice? Maybe the devil himself?"

"The devil cuts deals."

"Not this one."

The man put the revolver back in his pocket.

"You have three days."

The devil in Raybans turned and disappeared into the woods.

***

He lied.

"You're sure I won't be interrupting anything? I don't want to spoil your dinner."

"I live by myself, so don't worry. A little company isn't gonna kill me," Ms. Kingsley said over the phone.

Kenny nearly choked.

"Besides, if it's about Kyra, I'll do anything to help. You've got a wonderful little girl there, Mr. Perkins. She's one of my favs."

"You *are* Kyra's fav," Kenny said, trying to keep his voice even. He closed his eyes and squeezed the phone.

Ms. Kingsley let loose a giddy, girlish laugh. "Come on over anytime, Mr. Perkins. Me and Betty Crocker will be waiting for you."

He pictured her standing with one round hip up against the counter, a slender hand stirring a slow-cooked stew (did Betty Crocker make stew?), the strands of her youthful blond hair dangling at the edges of her neck, a stream of sunlight hazy in the kitchen window. Young, kind, exuberant, laughing, loving Ms. Kingsley. Kyra's favorite. Ever and ever.

He hung up the phone and ran to the bathroom and threw up his breakfast. And yesterday's dinner. And some of yesterday's lunch.

When it was over, he flushed the toilet, wiped his face, and rinsed out his mouth.

Staring at his haggard reflection in the bathroom mirror, he knew it was true. The day he killed Selma, he vomited up three days' worth of food. He was going to do it.

History repeats.

No. But it surely echoes.

***

Ms. Kingsley opened the door smiling. An oven mitt gloved her right hand. She was still dressed in her school clothes, but she'd unbuttoned the top of her blouse and washed the makeup off her face. She smelled young and fresh, like flowers blown by a warm wind in spring.

"Mr. Perkins."

"Kenny."

"Kenny! Come in. I was just pulling Ms. Crocker out of the oven."

"Smells fantastic."

"You shouldn't flatter. My mother was a wonder in the kitchen, a regular Paula Dean. But she passed all that to my sister. Me on the other hand, put me in an apron and hand me a spatula and I'm a wreck. I'll tear apart the kitchen, but there's never anything edible when I'm done."

She laughed, a sweet little bark that drilled into Kenny's ears and jolted something just below his navel. For a moment, he thought he was going to puke again. He gagged and coughed into his fist.

She led him down a hallway and into the kitchen. A steaming plastic oven tray sat on the counter. Vegetables and cheese and what looked to be small chunks of chicken.

"You have a wonderful house," Kenny said.

"It's too big. Some days I feel like all I do is work all day and come home and clean all night."

"I was surprised to hear you live here all alone. Pretty girl like you."

Ms. Kingsley sighed. "Actually, I *am* married, although it's just common law. Eight years. Doesn't seem that long until you say it."

"You never tied the knot? Officially?"

"We've never seen the need." She stabbed a knife through the thin membrane encasing her dinner. Steam poured out. "Not that we have anything against marriage."

Kenny shrugged.

With Selma, there had been time to plan. Time to ponder all the possibilities, the how and the when and the where. There had been time to navigate all that could go wrong. Here and now, with Ms. Kingsley (Mrs. Kingsley, apparently), there was no time at all. There was just the act, the doing of it, and a prayer that it wouldn't all fall apart.

"What was it you wanted to ask me about?"

Mrs. Kingsley tossed her oven mitt on the counter. Lifting the oven tray by her fingertips, she deposited it on a plate. Daintily she tore the plastic off the top of the tray and crumpled it into the trash. From a drawer, she removed a fork and spoon. The silverware rattled as the drawer slid shut.

"I just had a question or two," Kenny said. His mind raced. He had no questions.

She'll know. She'll realize something's wrong. She'll see that look on your face, black and full of murder. She'll scream. And scream. And scream.

"Shoot," Mrs. Kingsley said.

"I just wanted to know..."

The words trailed off as he glanced about the kitchen. Nothing here you wouldn't find in any other kitchen in America. Normal, everyday kitchenware.

The possibilities:

The set of kitchen knives in the wooden block. Two steps away, and then a knife in the hand. Three more steps and he'd be beside her. She wouldn't have time to do more than gasp before he plunged the blade into her. The air sucking out of her, and yank the blade back. Thrust. Out. Thrust. Out.

But so much blood.

Less obvious was the cutting board beside the knives. Two hands to hoist it up, and then close the distance fast and bring it down on the skull. She might get an arm in the air, and then there'd be the loud cracking snap of bone. Hoist the board again as she cried out. She wouldn't get a second chance to scream.

Blood again, though. And her skull—her pretty *face*—collapsed and sunken.

Beside him on the counter lay a thick dish towel, least likely of all. Wrapped around each hand and...

"Kenny? Mr. Perkins? You don't look so well."

Selma's face had risen unbidden in his mind, not as she had been for so much of her life—dusky, tan, beautiful—but as she was at the end: eyes bulging, wet hair whipped in a frenzy, a trail of bloody spittle running along her chin. And he remembered how he'd watched the life fade out of sight, the way you watch a balloon drift higher and higher until, finally, it disappears from view.

Selma. My devil has been long caged.

"You're not gonna be sick, are you? The bathroom's just down the hall."

"Just need to sit down."

"Here. Chair right behind you."

She stepped forward, reaching for the chair. He dove for her. At first she thought he was passing out. She tried to grab him, to hold him up. And then she realized the truth.

"Hey!"

He grabbed her by the waist and threw her. She crashed against the counter, her lower back jarring against the lip. A startled yelp burst out of her.

Kenny stepped in and punched her in the abdomen. The wind *whooshed* out of her. She collapsed, landing on her knees. A string of spit dangled from her mouth. In one quick motion he swung behind her, straddling her. He snatched at the dish towel. With two swift twirls he cinched it into a short length of rope.

And slipped it around her neck.

He rode her, yanking so hard her head bent back against his belly. Her eyes bulged, glaring up into his. Her hands snatched at the rag. A bright pink fingernail snapped off in the cloth. She heaved forward, and he stepped with her, keeping her firmly against him.

The devil come out. I hear him roaring.

Her face turned red, then blue, then purple. Her mouth opened, and he could see down her throat, the tongue and the jiggling glottis. Her hands slapped at him weakly now. Finally, they fell away. Her legs danced. A familiar smell filled the air.

Kenny waited, waited. He counted to one-twenty. Then he let her go. Her body slumped. Her head landed with a sickening smack against the floor.

Jesus.

He didn't know he was crying until he dropped the towel beside her body. She was dead.

He'd done it (again).

Mrs. Kingsley's lifeless bulging eyes glared at him. *I'm Kyra's favorite. Ever and ever. Who'll be her favorite now?*

He turned away.

He pulled the sleeve of his jacket over his hand and wiped the surface of everything he'd touched. Counter. Chair. Cutting board. He stepped over Mrs. Kingsley's body, wiping as he went.

Out of the kitchen and down the hall. Had he touched anything here? No. He didn't think so. He looked twice, just to be sure.

And he saw the pictures.

"What?" he whispered. "No no no no."

The pictures showed Mrs. Kingsley and, Kenny surmised, her common law husband. Mrs. Kingsley, young and sweet and innocent (and recently dead), and beside her

No no no no

the man in the black Raybans.

Kenny leaned forward, peering. There was no mistake.

What the hell is going on here? He blackmailed me to murder his wife?

The front door opened. A clopping of boots echoed down the hall.

"I just hope she's okay," came a voice. One Kenny recognized instantly. "When she called, she sounded so scared. She said the guy had been out in the lawn for over an hour."

"Let me go first," said another voice.

They were in the hall before Ken could move. The policeman, gun already drawn. Behind him, the man in the black Raybans. Except now his face was bare.

"Freeze!" the cop shouted. "Hands in the air! Now motherfucker!"

Kenny raised his hands.

"On your fucking knees! Now!"

Kenny saw the man—now without his Raybans—and the hot surging glee on his face.

"On your god damn knees!"

Kenny saw it all clearly. Saw how perfect it was. The real perfect crime.

"Hands on your head! Do it now!"

Perfect, except he didn't know the why.

"You killed her? You did it?" the man without the Raybans said.

Kenny put his hands on his head.

"Stay back," the cop said. "Just stay back."

Why? Why did you make me kill her?

"You did it?"

The man without the Raybans stepped forward into the light.

And when he did, Kenny saw something he hadn't noticed in the pictures. He stared into the man's eyes and found his answer.

The man's eyes were a dull, muddy brown.

The Waters and the Wild

GATES AWOKE one morning and knew the truth: his whole life was a mistake.

The realization struck like a hammer blow deep inside his brain, and a single word tolled within his skull: *failure, failure, failure.* He shook his head, but it wouldn't go away. Somewhere he'd gone off course, taken the wrong fork in the road, and now here he was, twenty or thirty or forty years later, an old man living all wrong, looking back and unable to see where the wrong began. He felt woozy, sick, the way a man feels after breaking to the surface from too deep a dive.

"Jeez!" he called.

Jeez, the butler, appeared. He held Gates' slippers and cotton robe.

"I've come to a realization, Jeez. Everything I've done is wrong."

"You are the most successful man in the world, sir," Jeez said. "Surely you've done something right."

Jeez rattled off the statistics: technological whiz kid and founder of Gates Tekk at twenty-one, multimillionaire at twenty-three, billionaire at twenty-five, major shareholder of Gates Global Conglomerate, three times Businessman of the Year, Forbes 500, cover of *Time*, *Newsweek*, the *New Yorker*...

"Stop, Jeez."

"But sir..."

"Enough. Look around you, Jeez."

Jeez looked. "A fine bedroom, sir."

"Yes, but *what* do you see?"

"Walls, sir?"

"Really *look*, Jeez. What do you see? Ionized titanium framing with synergistic heating and cooling tiles. High-density pixelated mycoplasma screens. Central ventilation system with purified mixtures of flavored aromas. Pine forest at seventy parts per million. Cinnamon, coffee bean, vanilla sprig, and mint leaf at thirty parts per million each. You can't even smell them distinctly, but they're there, Jeez, ticking off little sensors in the mind. Wake you up feeling giddy and spry. Different mixture at night to coax you into calm and peaceful sleep: sandalwood and apple smoke, chamomile and nutmeg, a tincture of moonbeam. All perfectly controlled by Mother."

"Your own design, sir."

Gates waved a hand. "You're missing the point, Jeez."

Gates snatched up a bedside remote and pointed at the wall. He clicked. The mycoplasma screen hummed and shimmered. The ocean shore appeared. Waves rolled in across a fine brown sand. A light mist clung along the horizon. The sun, a dense ball of fire, climbed towards heaven.

From hidden speakers came a light, tinkling sound: gurgling water, gulls bleating, wind rustling through high grass.

"I haven't seen the ocean in thirty years," Gates said.

"You see it every day, sir."

"I see *this*. *This* is not the ocean. This is what Mother *thinks* is the ocean."

"It looks real enough to me, sir."

"Does it? Are you sure? Does Mother have the right color of light on the horizon? The correct size of the grains of sand? Are those waves too large? Too small? What of those gulls? Do they really fly in that pattern, or is that only how Mother imagines they must fly? Has Mother calculated the right drafts of wind, the proper amount of salt spray in the air, the accurate flexibility of the grass?"

"You designed Her, sir. I'm sure She's perfect. But if you'd like confirmation, sir, I could send a boy down to the ocean right away."

Gates shook his head.

"Don't you see, Jeez? With the push of a button I've got the fake Cannon Beach in my bedroom. Another click and I've got the fake Kilimanjaro in my bathroom. *Click*. Fake *Mona Lisa* in the library. *Click*.

Fake *Last Supper* in the dining room. *Click.* Fake Dallas Cowboys cheer squad in the den. I'm the biggest faker in the history of the world."

Jeez's mouth puckered. He stared down at his polished shoes.

"Something must be done."

"What do you want done, sir?"

That was the question. Gates stood and pondered. For almost forty years he'd lived in the world's most perfect Home. He'd been coddled and swaddled and rocked to sleep by Mother for all that time. When he wanted something, he had it. Best of all, he never had to leave the House. Mother was everything. She cooked. She cleaned. She sang. And never, not once, did she complain. She was perfect in every way.

But for some time now Gates had been dully aware of a growing protuberance deep in his gut. A gnawing, rending sensation that woke him at odd hours and distracted his usually focused mind. An aching like hunger, but one unsatisfied by food.

A hunger of the soul.

"Sir?"

"I have an idea."

***

Gates told Alice at lunch.

"That sounds lovely, dear. Just lovely."

She'd been married to Gates twenty-five years and given him two beautiful children. More than once she'd stood with one ear tilted while Gates explained a plan that made her worry about his sanity. Early in their marriage she felt it her wifely duty to protest, to point out the obvious flaws and failings, to remind her husband that while she loved him dearly the rest of the world might not be so forgiving. She found this strategy never led where she wanted. Gates simply pushed on without her consent, and later he resented her. These days, Alice simply smiled, nodded, and told her husband what he wanted to hear. They were both happier that way.

"I'm sure it will be marvelous."

She offered Gates a tight little hug, wondering as she did how long she'd have to endure this current undertaking. She hoped it wouldn't disturb the fourth floor, which was exclusively her own.

"I've always thought the House needed a little more green."

Gates smiled. "That's just what we'll have."

The landscapers arrived at noon.

Gates stood on the front steps and bellowed so all could hear. "I want a wilderness! The grandest and most natural wilderness you've ever seen. I want jungle. I want swamp. I want river and waterfall. Whatever you see here right now, tear it up! Throw it out! And put in its place...*Mother Nature!*"

The back of the landscaper's trucks popped open. Inside was a whole new world. Inside were the Amazon, the Congo, the Himalayas, the Serengeti. There were redwood trees and coconut palms, cactus scrub and rubber saplings. There were blocks of ice and piles of shaved snow, river water and mountain streams, ocean silt and lake clay. One truck held wind from every continent. Another held shadows from every jungle. This was Mother Nature captured and bottled, ready to be sprung back into the world at a moment's notice.

Jeez supervised from the top of the steps. He held up a bullhorn and called out this way and that way, over here and over there. He pointed and shook his head, stamped his foot and pointed some more.

"And I want it inside," Gates said to Jeez.

"What's that, sir?"

"Inside. I want rainforest in the hallways. Meadows in the kitchen. A veldt in the library. When they're done out here, tell them to bring it inside."

Jeez's eyes rose, but he nodded swiftly. "As you wish, sir."

The next day the tigers arrived. They came in long rumbling trucks lined with cages. They were not alone. After the tigers came pumas and elephants, giraffes and gazelle, water buffalo and hippopotami. In the afternoon came the birds. Birds of every color and every size, squawking and whistling and cawing and chirping. Birds that talked. Birds that sang. Birds danced the tango and formed a line to conga. They were everywhere.

More arrived that evening:

A pride of lions.

A herd of zebra.

A coil of pythons.

A pack of hyena.

A sleuth of black bears.

A colony of army ants.

A raft of wild ducks.

A mob of kangaroos.

On and on they came.

"Where shall we put them all?" Jeez asked.

"Let them run wild," Gates said. "That is why they're here. I want Nature, Jeez. Raw and red in the tooth. Let them run. Let them do as they please."

"But they'll surely kill each other, sir."

"That's Mother Nature, Jeez. She's mean and She's cruel, but She's fair. There's a dangerous beauty to Her, and I've not looked Her in the eye for far too long."

Jeez let the animals out of their cages. They flowed like living a river, pulsing out of their bounds and streaming into the newly formed jungles and the pristine plains. Within minutes they disappeared, finding new homes amongst the Gates Estate. All that remained was a single elephant butting its head against the front door.

"Knock it down," Gates said. "If it wants in, let it in."

"But sir!"

"There are no doors in Nature, Jeez. Knock it down."

A buzzing noise came from the Intercom by the door. Gates pushed the button.

"Yes, darling?"

"I need to speak with you right now," sparked Alice's voice from the ComLink.

"Of course," Gates said.

"Right...now."

Gates glanced up towards the fourth floor window.

"Coming."

***

Gates listened patiently.

"I've had just about enough of this. You told me this was only going to go so far. A little *remodeling* you said. A few new *plants* you said. Some *pets* you said."

Gates nodded emphatically. Yes, yes, and yes.

"There is *dirt* in my hallways! There are...*vines*! Earlier today, I found a *gazelle* in my bathroom. In my *bathroom*! Using my *facilities*! I won't stand for it. I am your wife, and I have rights. I won't stand for this any longer."

Gates waited until he was certain her fury had calmed.

"Darling, don't you see that I am doing this for us? Don't you see that we've built up this bubble all around us for years and years and years? A bubble of glass and metal and silicon and high-speed optical fiber. We've built it and lived inside it and it's made us unhappy and cold and lonely. And why? Because we don't actually talk, we squawk through the Com-Link. We don't cook, we order food from the AutoChef. I haven't seen your real face in years, darling. I've only seen what that Beauty Wizard has made you into. Not my wife. Just hair spray and eye liner and mascara and nail polish all applied by an artificial intelligence. It's all the bubble, Ally. And I'm tired of it. I'm tearing it down."

Alice stood speechless for a long time.

"You want me to go without makeup?"

"I want you to be you."

"What about my hair? My wrinkles? George, I have *wrinkles*."

"You'll be all natural again."

"You're insane."

Gates sighed. He turned to his children, who waited patiently on the bed.

"Adam! Alicia!"

"Daddy!"

"Today we pop the bubble. I want you to throw away your clothes! Mess up your hair! Run through the jungle! Play and be free!"

"Yeah!"

"No clothes!"

"Yeah!"

"No shoes!"

"Yeah!"

"Do we have to take baths?"

"Never again!" Gates cried.

"Yeah!"

"Do we have to eat our vegetables?"

"Eat whatever you find on the trees, my darlings."

"Yeah!"

"Go! Be wild!"

The children scampered off the bed and down the hall and out of sight.

"I won't do it," Alice said quietly.

Gates took her hand. "When did you start believing that you ever needed perms and eye shadow and lip gloss and facial creams to make you beautiful? You are naturally beautiful. Just as God made you."

Alice looked down. "You really think so?"

"Yes, darling."

"You wouldn't lie?"

"Never."

Alice threw her arms around him. "I love you."

"I love you."

"I'll try. For you, George."

"There's nothing like it. Trust me. Soon it will be perfect. Real and live and wild. Mother Nature. The way we've always supposed to live. We'll live like God intended. We'll pick fruit from the trees. We'll lay under the shade of palms. We'll feel wind on our bare backs and clean water between our toes. We'll do it all. And you know what?"

"What?"

"We'll be the happiest people on Earth."

***

Something was wrong.

"The feeling in my gut, Jeez," Gates said. "It hasn't budged."

"Perhaps you need a laxative, sir."

"No, something's *missing*. It's like we've gorged on potato chips. Empty calories. No sustenance at all. And at the end, we're still hungry. That's what we have here, Jeez. Emptiness. Hunger."

"But how, sir?"

Gates' dark eyes narrowed. "We have made only pseudo-nature. We've fallen short of the real thing."

"But, sir!"

"Look at how the leaves droop in the halls. Watch how the tigers lounge all day by the pools. The gorillas do nothing but fart and scratch. This rain...ha! It does not pour. It drizzles. The river does not rush. It meanders. Do you smell this air, Jeez?"

Jeez sniffed. He thought it smelled pretty rank.

"Pungent?" Gates asked. "Hardly. This is not Mother Nature's air. We've been had, Jeez."

"But this is everything you wanted, sir."

"It's wrong. All wrong. We must set it right."

"How, sir?"

"We must make it more natural."

Jeez sniffed the air again and wondered if, once the air was more natural, he might not need a nose plug.

"You cannot do Mother Nature halfway, Jeez. This is a test of our resolve. And we must meet this test. We must make nature more natural. That is our goal now."

Jeez shuddered. Already a thick layer of black soil carpeted every hall. Damp rains fell in nearly every room (save the Sahara Room, where rain *never* fell). Blustery winds carried from the Kilimanjaro Room directly through the Yellowstone Kitchen, making for wintry lunches and frosty dinners. Jeez himself had twice been pawed by a stealthy black puma that roamed the House. And there was simply no sleeping for all the cawing birds and buzzing insects. There was no peace in the House any longer.

"Get Dowin on the phone," Gates said.

"Yes, sir," Jeez said faintly, without resolve.

The ComLink had been shut off days before. Jeez took out his personal cell phone, dialed, and handed over the phone.

"Dowin here, Gates' Genetics Division."

"Dowin, this is Gates."

"Sir."

"I need you, son."

"Of course, sir. Anything, sir."

"I need genetically modified fertilizer. The plants here are all limp and saggy. The vines don't cling. They just hang like limp string. I want more perk, Dowin. I want plants that stand at attention, that snap and grab and jostle when you go by. The bigger, greener, and leafier the better. I want plants that remind you why civilized man never ventured into the depths of Africa. Understand?"

"Can do, sir."

"And the animals are all a wash. The zoo has lamed their instinct. You've never seen a lazier bunch of butt sniffers. The other day I told Jeez to stick his head in the lion's mouth. He could have laid it there and taken a nap."

"We can do genetic modification, sir. Clone you a whole new set."

"Perfect. I want them wild, Dowin. No kittens and goldfish, understand? Red in tooth and claw, that's what we're after. The real Mother Nature."

"I could get you a saber-tooth tiger, sir."

"Make it two. And snappy."

"Already ordered, sir."

"And the air, Dowin."

"What about it, sir?"

"This isn't Mother Nature's air, son. It smells like a dying circus. The ocean air needs more salt and tide. The mountain air needs more pine and sky. The arctic air needs more ice and desolation. Right now it's just all wrong."

"I'm calling an Eskimo right now, sir. I'll have him step outside and get you a whiff."

"Excellent."

"Anything else, sir?"

"I need something for myself. All these colognes and aftershaves and deodorants have built up for five decades. They're in my pores. In my DNA. I need a body spray. Something that really reeks."

"Tangy and obscene, sir? Heavy dose of swampy feet and unwashed body hair?"

"That's the stuff."

"Not a problem, sir."

"Good man."

Gates hung up the phone.

He felt better already.

***

It didn't take long.

Dowin's improvements arrived the next day. Trucks from Gates' Genetics Division lined up in the driveway, and from morning until late evening they unloaded their wild cargo. Gates stood on the porch, nodding and smiling and clapping his hands.

The Sprayers came first. They wore dim green suits and carried heavy silver canisters on their backs. Narrow hoses snaked from the canisters to long thin rods the Sprayers held in their hands. They shuffled from the trucks across the lawn into the House and everywhere about the property. They sprayed and sprayed.

The foliage thickened. Plants stretched up as if waking from a long slumber. Leaves grew greener. A thick mucus dripped from limbs and stalks. New flowers blossomed in a matter of hours, each bud a raging, virulent color that stung the eye.

After the Sprayers came the new animals.

Saber-tooth tigers with nine inch claws.

Komodo dragons that spit funnels of fire.

Pterodactyls six feet high with wings that stank of death.

A python eighty feet long.

Dowin's animals sprang from their cages. They roared and clawed and hissed and screeched. They snapped and pounced and mangled and swiped. They broke free in their hundreds and swarmed across the Estate, and everywhere they went a scream rose up. The new ate the old. The law of the jungle reigned.

Gates marveled at what he saw.

Mother Nature.

In all her glory.

***

Something wasn't right.

Gates couldn't put his finger on it. Dowin had come through brilliantly. Everything had been perfect: the animals, the plants, the air. All of it exactly as Gates wanted. Then why was there still this ache in his gut?

Something was wrong.

Some small detail had escaped him. Something infinitesimal, but important. You couldn't fake Mother Nature, Gates knew that. And you couldn't fool your gut. You either had it *exactly right,* or you didn't have it at all.

Gates stared out his bedroom window at the New World he'd created. Where had he gone wrong? He heard the howls and cries of his kingdom in the night. Was it the New Breed? He breathed the cool dank air. Was it the air? He peered into the gloomy darkness. Was it the quality of light?

His gut roiled.

Gates knew what had to be done.

***

For three days Gates locked himself away in his room.

He experimented with the air. To the humidifiers, he added droplets of salt spray, draughts of black tar, tinctures of oleander and mint. He aerosolized a mixture of bone and feces and moth wings and sprayed it into every crevice. At night he gathered cobwebs and bat droppings, nightcrawlers and owl feathers, which he burned in a heap to catch the smoke in a beaker. When it had cooled, he blew the smoke upon the curtains.

During the day he was a student of light. He strained sunrise and sunset through tinted filters and recorded every shade and hue. From Gates Laboratories he ordered bulbs in every color, screwing them in at random along the ceiling, in lamps, in flashlights upon the floor. A rainbow of light cut crisscross throughout the room.

Rain he had shipped from every corner of the globe. He had a monsoon from India, a flood from Argentina, a rapid from the Congo, a drizzle from the Swiss Alps. Each he distilled, recording exact chemical makeups, temperatures, consistencies. He mixed them, boiled them, stirred them and whirred them, seeking out their watery secrets.

Three days and nights the experimenting continued. The door never unlocked. No one came. No one went.

And then, on the fourth morning, the bedroom door opened.

A voice issued forth:

"Jeez! Bring my family."

Gates' clothes were in tatters, his shirt gone entirely and flapping shreds of his pants dangling at his ankles. The hair on his chest was singed black. He was bald. A dark streak ran along his arm the color of dried blood. But it was his eyes that worried Jeez most. They were the eyes of a man who'd looked too long at the stars, looked and looked until he'd seen something beyond them, something man was never meant to see.

"Good heavens, sir."

"I've done it, Jeez."

"Are you alright, sir? You haven't eaten in three days. You need a meal, sir. A meal and a bath."

"I've made it right, Jeez. It's finally right. Bring Alice and the kids. They have to see. They have to see what I've done."

"But, sir..."

"Bring them now, Jeez."

Jeez brought them.

"George, my god!"

"I've done it, darling."

"Look at you!"

"Daddy!"

"It's over, now," Gates said. "You must come and see."

Gates held out his hand.

The children took a hand each.

"You look terrible, Daddy."

"Daddy's just tired. He's worked very hard."

Alice shook her head. "You're scaring them, George. Scaring me, too."

"There's nothing to fear. It's finally done. Come look."

Alice followed her husband and children through the door.

Jeez came last, but he stopped at the doorway and put only his head inside.

"My god."

Inside the bedroom, the ionic mycoplasma screens had been revived. They were different now. Gates had manually adjusted their settings. A sweltering jungle appeared on every screen, and a dense canopy up above. Heaps of soil and plants and trees lay scattered through the room, and they blended seamlessly into the images on the screens. Lights from above winked and flickered, and the screens appeared to pulse with the light. A misty fog twined along the edge of the screens, but it also appeared to rise out from the floor.

Jeez bent down and wiped his hand through the fog. His fingers came away wet.

"Sir?" Jeez called.

He could no longer see the Gates family clearly. They were now only dark outlines at the far end of the room. The faltering chatter of the children drifted through the heavy air.

"Sir!"

Jeez watched. He rubbed his eyes. He thought the fog must be affecting his sight, because he was certain he'd just seen the Gates family step past the last clump of trees and *into* the mycoplasma screen.

Impossible.

Jeez shook his head.

They were still going, fading now, into the screen. Wavering, darkening, gone.

"Sir?" Jeez whispered.

And from somewhere in the wild, the screaming began.

Not Dead, Not Even Past

THIS MONDAY MORNING at Village Mart I saw the dead boys in the produce isle. It wasn't the first time, but the name of the one beside the cilantro and parsley escaped me. They stood like pale statues, gritty water dripping from their sodden clothes and slicking the gray tile, and when the misters came on the faint spray coated the carrots and celery and peppers and passed right through the dead boys. I looked away toward the back of the store. Bill, the manager, gave me a wave.

"Anything I can do you for, Sheriff?"

"Fine, Bill. Just fine."

"Rough year, huh? Can't remember one like this, and I been here a long stretch of years."

I couldn't either.

When I turned back, the dead boys were gone.

I finished shopping. Getting back in my car, the name came back to me. I took out my notepad and wrote:

Vincent Raines, nine years old. Row twelve. Drowned. Body unrecovered.

I put the notepad in the dash. I didn't want to forget.

They were getting closer.

***

On Tuesday we had another floater.

Deputy Rick Brenner perched on the hillside along Highway 7 with an aluminum pole used to clean out swimming pools. He'd taken half a dozen swings at the bobbing body, but had come up short each time. When the pole splashed short once again, he gave me a strained look and a spat on the ground.

"I gotta get lower," he hollered.

I stood at the top of the hill along the road and gave him a nod.

The kid took two lurching steps down the hillside. On the second, the dirt slid out from under him. He stumbled, his left foot landing with a splash in the water. He cursed and shook his head, but he stayed put.

The first swing of the pole didn't gain purchase, but he hooked the floater with the second. Brenner grunted loudly, gave a hard tug and pulled the floater into shore. The kid kept two hands on it, pulling with his legs as he came back up the hill, but the pole slid loose as the floater came close. He let the pole drop and reached for the body.

He caught it along the wrist. Another sharp grunt, and then the kid was on his ass on the hillside. A puff of dirt rose around him. He stared at the hand which had only a moment ago held the floater's wrist. In it was a gunky white clump of flesh and tissue. It took a moment for the truth to settle in, and then the kid was stabbing his arm into the water and thrashing it around, trying to wash it clean while he retched up his breakfast.

I dropped my Marlboro onto the ground and stubbed it with my heel. Across Lake Chelan, the sun was rising like a hot red eye. A warm spring air rustled the tops of the trees. It was too nice a day to do such gruesome work.

A battered Chevy Biscayne pulled onto the shoulder. I walked slowly to it. Mrs. Whitesand rolled down the window as I approached.

"Everything alright, Sheriff?" She tilted her sunglasses down the bridge of her nose.

A dead boy sat in the backseat.

(*Henry Boggs, fifteen years old. Starting linebacker. Drowned. Body unrecovered*)

"Everything's fine, Betty. Nothing to see here."

"They work you too hard, Sheriff. This year harder than most. You want me to bring you some apple pie? I baked two for the kids, but Russel decided he wasn't coming for the weekend, and I can't very well eat one all on my own. Got my figure to watch, you know."

Her eyes never caught my own. They seemed to lean forward of their own accord, like heavy marbles dangling precariously upon her face.

The dead boy put a hand to the window. Beneath him, Mrs. Whitesand's backseat was soaking.

"Better move along, Betty."

"Well, alright. You don't want that pie?"

"You bring it to the station whenever you got time."

"Take care, Sheriff."

She steered carefully back onto the road. As she pulled away, I saw the backseat was now empty.

Below, Brenner got himself under control. He looped the end of the pole through the floater's belt and lodged the other end beneath a rock. He kicked it twice to make sure it wouldn't budge. Then he came back up the hill.

"Tell Alvin I'm sorry," the kid said. "I didn't think, you know? Guy's whole hand just...just..."

The kid looked like wax. I thought he might lose it again. There wasn't no shame in it. I'd lost it plenty of times myself. But he took a deep breath and let it out slow.

"Hope it don't make no difference for Alvin."

Alvin was the medical examiner. I told him I didn't see that it would, not unless the floater slit just his one wrist and bled himself to death before jumping into the cold clear water of Lake Chelan. Which didn't seem likely.

"It's Fred Durnam, ain't it?"

I looked. "Looks like it. He always wore suspenders."

"Damn it."

"What'd you think we was gonna find? He's been missing four days. Found his boat, empty, Thursday morning."

A disappointed look settled on the kid's face, like someone had told him the truth about Santa Claus when he wasn't quite ready to accept it.

"I just thought maybe he took off. Went to Vegas or something. Found a younger woman. I don't know." He waved his hand at the lake. "Not this."

He was a good kid. Better, he was a good cop. Those are two separate things, not always found in the same package. I'd known plenty of good men who'd make lousy cops, and more than one good cop I'd worked with had made a mess of things at home. And there were cases like my own: a decent cop too worried about how badly he'd screw up a home life he didn't even bother to try. I came close to marriage once. Dodged that bullet, as they say, but now I was getting to an age that I wondered if I'd taken the path of lesser resistance only to find that it lead to the greater mistake. I had no children, and lately—since I'd hired Brenner, really—I'd lain awake a few nights a week asking myself just what I was leaving behind. If it was going to be anything worthwhile, it'd have to be something cop, because I sure as hell didn't have any home wisdom.

Which may have explained why I'd kept Brenner on after I discovered his story didn't check out. He said he hailed from up Okanogan way. His father was a cherry farmer. His mother ran off when he was ten. He hadn't exactly been aces in school, and when graduation came it was either the service or the academy. Way he told it, if he was going to get shot he'd rather have it happen close to home.

I don't pry into a man's personal life. But it is my job to ask questions about an officer's professional history. In Brenner's case, there wasn't much. He was fresh out of the academy. But when the academy instructor called—he'd had a kid by that name, sure, real fine officer material, you bet, but that was 1972 and maybe I needed to double-check my dates— I knew I had a problem. I didn't take to having my chain pulled. But...

He was a natural cop. He looked at a man and had a sharp, quick instinct that parceled lies from truth. He smelled crime the way a dog smells piss on a tree. It came to him, like stink in the wind, and he followed his sense down alleys and around corners until, like magic, he stumbled upon thieves, arsonists, and violent offenders. I'd seen it, and it never ceased to amaze me. After two weeks training the kid, I let him drive. He never steered me wrong. It was more than that, though. Every cop knows you spend enough time in a bad neighborhood, you're gonna kick over a trash can sooner or later and out will spill something you didn't want on your shoe. It was the way he handled himself. Most rookies, you watch their hand always quivering near their holster. Itching. The kid used one weapon, and so far he hadn't needed any other. He talked. It was something in the tone of his voice, the way it brought you down softly, made you forget all the terrible, criminal things you were in the mind of doing in that one hot moment. He never raised it, but that voice of his was some kind of force.

I had me a long, hard think. He wasn't a murderer or some child rapist. I'd run his fingerprints and he had no criminal record. But there was the lie about the academy, and where there was one lie there were generally more. They bred like maggots.

In the end, I let it stand. We're all running from something. That's the way I saw it. And if you put me on the stand and asked me did I do it because he was a good cop or did I do it because I'd started—in only two months' time—to think of him as a son, well I don't know what kind of answer I could give you. An honest one would have to be a bit of both.

But mostly he was a good kid.

"We wait for Alvin?"

I shook my head. "He'll be here soon enough. We got someplace we gotta be."

"Wherever we're going can't wait ten minutes?"

"It's been waiting twenty-five years, kid. I think it's done waiting."

He frowned at that, but he knew better than to ask. Which was good.

I wasn't ready to tell.

***

Vera Stanton lived in a ramshackle two-story at the end of Purtleman Gulch Road. Her nearest neighbor was three miles off. She'd once been a prominent woman in town, had even run for mayor before her husband left her and her two kids flew away to east coast schools, never to return. She'd sold her husband's property and bought a rickety, weather-beaten heap far out of town. Beneath the crooked rows of baby-blue shingles grew an immense garden that stretched from the edge of the house to the ditch along the road, a wandering, tangled mess of weeds and vines that had broken out of bounds and spiraled out of control, much like Vera Stanton's life. I'd known Vera for twenty-five years. I hadn't spoken to her in twenty-four of them.

We parked next to a gray Volkswagen van. I left the engine running. If all went well, this wouldn't take long.

Vera stood on the porch as we crossed the gravel strip to her front door. She held a dish towel in one hand, the other rested on the screen door. Some people age well, so that if you catch them in the right light you can see clearly who they'd been when they were younger. You almost wonder if the heavy lines of age, the little sags of skin, the dark half-moons under the eyes are not all just some thin and flimsy costume ready to be discarded, the true and healthy person waiting underneath. Vera Stanton wasn't one of those people. She wore her age like a heavy cloak. Her shoulders sunk. Her back bowed. The white wisps of her hair clung to her head like so many dry and strangled weeds. Only her eyes had any life, and she focused them on me now.

"Sheriff Crawford," she said. "I know why you're here, and you can go away. I don't need your advice or your company."

"Fred Durham's dead," I said. "We just fished him out of the lake. Alvin Neil is cutting him open right now as we speak." Alvin was doing no such thing. If anything, he was still driving Fred's body out to Wenatchee where a proper autopsy could be done. But I'd heard the steel in Vera's voice, and if I was going to get her to listen I needed to take that steel away.

"Fred Durham," Vera said slowly. Her eyes narrowed slightly, but there was no surprise there. "George's boy."

I nodded. "Alvin's doing what he does, Vera, but we both know what he's going to find, don't we? You and me? We know."

"I suspect he'll find Fred's lungs are full of water."

"Just like Kaity Pritchet's. And Jason Yardley's."

Vera waved the towel in our direction as if shooing flies. "You're on my property, Sheriff. I advise you to get off it. You're trespassing." She turned to go back inside.

"Don't forget Blake Yardley. And Hannah Porter. And her sister Lindsey. And Alison Poirer. There's fourteen of them, Vera. Fourteen. You think that's an accident?"

She paused behind the screen. "What do you want from me?"

"You've got to tell them."

For a moment, the old woman said nothing. She took a long, wheezing breath and looked past me to Brenner, who hadn't budged from the front of the cruiser. She seemed to study the kid. I couldn't tell if she liked what she saw.

"My children left me long ago," Vera said at last. "They spend their holidays with their father. Once in a while, they send me a card. They think my birthday is July 25th. Why bother to correct them? What good do you think it would do, Cal? They're crazy old coot of a mother calling them up, raving wild stories in their ears? How would you take it, if it was one of your kids?" She stopped and gave a little huff. "But you don't have any, do you? Lucky."

"You have to tell them," I said again.

She shook her head. "It's been a sad year for the valley, Cal. I won't deny that. But you're jumping to conclusions."

"Fourteen suicides," I said. "In five months. And there'll be three more to finish it."

"The economy," she offered.

I repeated the names to her. The edge of her mouth twitched at each one, like she was biting her tongue at the crack of a whip.

"Very sad," she said. "But meaningless."

She opened her door and stepped inside.

I tromped up the porch steps. I grabbed the screen before she could shut it.

"Fred Durham called in about kids at night," I said in a low voice, catching her eyes with mine. "He never saw them, but he heard them. Late at night, early morning. Thought they were local kids making mischief. Knocking over trash cans, throwing rocks at windows. Petty stuff. He called twice. Have you heard any kids out here at night?"

Her breath hiccupped in her throat. Wide, startled eyes blinked and focused beyond me, through the door and into her yard.

"You've seen them," I said.

"I've seen nothing. There's no one out here but me."

"You *have* seen them. I've seen them, too. At first I thought it was just...waking nightmares. But I see them more and more. You do, too, don't you?"

"I don't know what you're talking about, Sheriff. What you see is your own affair. It's got nothing to do with me."

"Vincent Raines," I said. "Henry Boggs. Leonard McCalister. You know who I'm talking about."

Her head shook violently back and forth. "Get off my property, Sheriff. Stop harassing an old woman."

She swept back and shut the door.

I let the screen fall shut and went back to the car. Brenner gave me a wondering stare.

"Cheery conversation," he said.

As we pulled out of the driveway, I spotted the dead man by the mailboxes across the road. He held his hat in his hand. With the other, he stuck out his thumb.

(*Glenn Harper, forty-seven years old. Father of Becky Harper. Body found*)

His eyes tracked the cruiser as we turned away from him. He bucked his thumb up and down, begging for a ride, but I didn't stop. The way he was heading was a dead end.

***

There was plenty of paperwork to do when we got back to the station. I gave it to the kid. He took it and sat at his desk and went to work. He didn't look up for three hours. I went to my office and closed the door.

In a small town like Chelan, the emergency lines were always open, but the police station itself kept regular hours. We closed at six every evening. It was nearing closing when Brenner opened the door and poked his head inside. I motioned for him to enter.

"What's goin on here, boss? What was that this afternoon?"

There were times when he looked too young to be doing this job, just a kid. His face hadn't fully lost the round, boyish plump of youth. His hair still held a shine, and it grew thickly across his forehead. Enough years in this job and that was all likely to change, but then it all had to go eventually. You didn't outrun life. Right now he more closely resembled the man he was growing into. Somber. Analytical. Shrewd. Sometimes it looked like this were a role he was playing, one he wasn't yet comfortable with, but I knew that one day he would wear it like an old suit. But I wouldn't be around to see it.

"She knew you."

I nodded. "We were involved together years ago."

"Romantically?"

"No. We were on a board together. I was very young then. Younger than you."

"You worked together. For the sheriff's department?"

"This isn't the place for this conversation, kid."

"Where is?"

"You really want to know this?"

"Boss, something's goin on here. Not just today, and not just up Purtleman Gulch. Fourteen suicides in five months? And you seem to know what the hell it's all about, but for some reason you ain't telling me. Yeah, I want to know."

I got up. "Okay then. Let's take a ride."

***

I parked the cruiser on the south shore of Lake Chelan, some seven miles uplake. Another few miles the road wound to the state park, but along here there was nothing but a wide patch of gravel and a sharp drop into the cold blue water. At this end the deep canyon that held Lake Chelan rose up sharply and formed a shallow basin. Average depth was thirty-five feet. But here the basin had dropped off, and the dark water covered the edge of a sharp, steep cliffside that shot to a depth of seven hundred feet. Miles uplake that number seemed puny. At its deepest, Lake Chelan was twice that deep.

"This is where it happened," I said.

The kid looked at me, then out to the lake. He waited patiently. It was a beautiful view, the calm stretch of water and the summer homes on the far shore. The sun dropped along the horizon like a coin falling into a slot.

"Twenty-five years ago," I said. "Sometimes I wake up and think to myself, how the hell has it been that long? I got pictures from back then I look at and think, that ain't me, I don't know that guy at all. I don't know what he was thinking, what he was doing, why the hell he made any of the decisions he did. It ain't me. Course, I know better. That's me, alright. Just not the same me, the me I am now. And I think the me I am now would do things differently. But maybe I'm fooling myself. Maybe that's just a lie I tell myself to get to sleep."

"You're talking about when you were on the board with Ms. Stanton."

"We were on the school board together. Funny, ain't it? Vera was quite the politician back then, had her sights on city council and mayor. I thought that's where I was headed, too, but you couldn't go that way without any experience. The school board was an easier start, not the job itself, necessarily, but getting elected. There weren't many people running against you.

"I was the youngest member of the board. There were seven of us, in case of a tie. Vera was the head of the board. I was the lowest ranking member, being how I was youngest. I only served that one year. I was supposed to serve four, that was the term, but I stepped down after one. After it happened. After the accident."

I pulled out my pack of Marlboros. I lit a cigarette and rolled down the window. The kid turned and looked out at the dying sun.

"The way it happened it was early morning on February twenty-first. It snowed the night before, but the plows had been out and the roads were clear when the buses started out. It started snowing again about seven o'clock, and the calls went out to the schools to let them know some of the buses might pull in late. But no worries, the kids would all get there eventually.

"Bus 29 was driven by Oliver Thomas. He was only a part-time bus driver. He was a part-time everything, really. Bus driver. Mechanic. Husband. Father. Only two things Oliver Thomas did full-time was coach football and drink. Most places, most times, the kind of drinking Oliver Thomas did wouldn't be left alone. Even here in good old Chelan it wouldn't, except for one thing: Oliver Thomas won football games. He was the winningest football coach in the history of Chelan Goats football. Nine straight playoff appearances. Three state title games. No trophies yet, but everyone knew one was coming. Had to be. It was destiny. You looked into Coach Thomas's eyes and that's what you believed. He knew it and you knew it and you both believed it like you believed in God or gravity. So the drinking...well, every man's got his burden.

"Ralph Kellar ran the bus garage in those days, and he claimed later that Oliver Thomas came to work sober, bright-eyed and bushy-tailed. Said they'd had a good talk that very morning, that Oliver had told him some fine jokes, and the man got into his bus and went away happy, smiling and content with the world. Which sounded good when Ralph told it to the investigative committee, but which everyone who knew Oliver knew was a bloody damn lie. Oliver Thomas wasn't ever happy or content with anything, not unless he was three-sheets to the wind and driving up the lead on Friday night.

"The truth was likely that Oliver was drunk but functioning, chewing on aspirin and sucking down coffee straight and black. He was more likely to be giving Ralph the finger than telling any jokes, but what we know for sure is that he left the bus garage on time that morning and picked up his first ten stops on time. April Harper would later confirm that Oliver was running five minutes behind when he reached the Harper residence. Her husband, Glenn, accompanied their daughter to school each morning. He was a janitor for the high school.

"The last stop Bus 29 made that morning was at the home of Nicholas Varner. Nick's mother stated later that she had a bad premonition that morning. She'd woken up out of a bad dream and thrown up in her toilet. She said that happened only once before, when her sister died in a plane accident. Nobody much took that seriously, but it's what she said. The Varner stop was nearly ten minutes late, and by then the snow was coming down good and hard.

"In the official report, it was declared that icy road conditions and limited visibility were the main contributing factors in Bus 29 leaving the roadway and plunging over the embankment into the lake. We knew better. All of us did. You didn't need a weather map to know which way the wind blows, as Bob Dylan once said. Even after he escaped that sinking bus and crawled onto shore, Oliver Thomas was still staggering drunk. The chill took a lot of that out of him, but Sheriff Bainer said later—not to the official investigative committee, of course—that you could still smell the reek of liquor on the man's breath when they put him in the ambulance.

"Nine kids and one adult came out of the water that morning. Sixteen kids and one adult did not. Trained rescue divers combed the lake for weeks, but Bus 29 and twelve of its victims were never found. One diver came up saying he thought he'd spotted the bus, but he must have been mistaken. He said he thought he'd seen the headlights flashing under the water, but that was after three weeks of searching, and clearly the man was imagining things.

"The investigative committee was made up of various local officials, but in the end it had only the power to make recommendations to the school board. The police department chose not to file any charges against Oliver, and this left the school board with the final decision regarding any kind of discipline."

I took a long drag of the cigarette and then flicked it out the window.

"We voted unanimously to let Coach Thomas continue on as head coach of the Goats. His license as a district bus driver was revoked, but aside from that he was free and clear. It was felt at the time that this was an adequate punishment. After all, didn't he already have the weight of seventeen deaths on his conscience? What good would taking football away from him do, for him or for the community? So we let him be. He coached for seventeen more years. No championships, that always eluded us. But he's still the winningest coach in Goats history."

"What does any of that have to do with these suicides now?"

"The board members were myself, Vera, and Adam Poirer, Michael Pritchard, Eli Porter, Jonathan Yardley, and Kaitlin Nelson."

The kid's hand went to his mouth. For a long while, the car was silent.

"It's all their kids, isn't it?"

I nodded. "Their kids and grandkids."

"Fourteen of them."

"Seventeen people died in that wreck, kid. That leaves three more. Vera's got two kids of her own, no grandkids though."

"But surely they can't all be..."

"You've seen the reports. Nine floaters. Three hangings. Two shooters. And what links them all?"

"They all had water in their lungs."

"Even the ropers and the shooters. Water in the lungs."

"It's impossible."

"No," I said, shaking my head. "It's justice."

***

Saturday morning I got the call from the east coast. Hank and Linda Stanton had taken a boat out onto Lake Carlsbad Friday for a nice, quiet row. The boat floated up on shore the next morning, minus its passengers. They'd sent out search and rescue. They're hopes were high.

They found the bodies that afternoon.

***

When they find my body, many will ask why. He wasn't that old, they'll say. He had it all together. Never seemed like the type. And they'd be right.

But some will know.

Vera Stanton, for one, if she ever recovers from her stroke. They took her down to Wenatchee Valley Hospital, but Dr. Thayer tells me there's a good chance she'll be back to her old self in no time. Physically, anyway. Mentally, well...

But she'll know. And maybe the kid will understand. I hope he will.

I'm doing it for him.

If I had anything to tell him, I'd tell him you can't escape the past. You can bury it, run from it, pretty it up, but the past has a way of lingering, the way the odor of cigarette smoke clings to your walls. You can scrub all you want. You can change the wallpaper. But that stink is always there. It's with you forever.

I drove my personal car out here tonight. Someone will call it in early in the morning. They'll find me tomorrow, unless I'm never found at all. I decided to wear jeans, a T-shirt, boots. I didn't want to do it in my uniform.

For a while I stand on the rocks and gaze into the water. I know they're out there. I can feel them. They are waiting for me.

I ease into the cold black water of Lake Chelan. The boots are heavy, but it doesn't matter. I won't be swimming long. I take long strokes and kick hard. In a short distance, I've grown tired. I slow and tread water.

The stars above twinkle, and I remember that their light has traveled thousands and thousands of light years to reach Earth, that the stars I see now may no longer even exist, that they may have winked out long ago in their own galaxies but that we won't know for many years to come. It is the past I'm staring at, the past still existing in the present.

When I glance down at first I think I'm seeing the reflection of the stars in the water. But the lights below are growing brighter, larger.

And then I see their faces.

Their blank, dead eyes.

And I feel their hands.

I take a deep breath.

The Other Side of the Door

THE YOUNG MAN stood at the door leading to the other half of the duplex. Mrs. Hardy watched him fiddling with the rusted brass knob, twisting it this way and that the way a small boy will, testing it with the infantile certainty that if he just keeps it up the result will change. It was a rather cute quality in a boy of five, not so amusing in a full grown man.

"What was that?" Mrs. Hardy asked.

"The key? Where's the key to this door?"

She was trying to remember the young man's name. A plain and simple name, she knew, not like most of the horrid, cantankerous names people saddled their kids with these days. A plain and simple name which matched his rather plain and simple face. Not an unattractive face, but only one who's individually attractive qualities—wispy blond hair, square chin, light hint of rugged stubble—did not seem to add up to any greater attractiveness. Mrs. Hardy glanced down at the lease agreement. David. There it was.

"There is no key. I thought I mentioned that earlier."

The young man's hand left the knob. A tiny smear of disgust wavered along his upper lip, as if he'd come across a mess left by an untrained house pet. He dug his hands down into his pockets.

"I can check with Mr. Frank about the key, but far as I know there isn't one. Not in the twenty years I've been letting the place. But there's no need to worry. Mr. Frank never rents both sides at once. You'll have the place here to yourselves."

"Don't worry about it."

Mrs. Hardy had already determined the young man didn't like the house. Which really was no matter, for there was the girl, and Mrs. Hardy focused her energies on her. It was Mrs. Hardy's opinion, gleaned from a lifetime in real estate, that it was the woman who chose the house. The man merely stood with his hands in his pockets and waited for the decision to be made.

The girl was upstairs. Mrs. Hardy listened to her bustling about, tramping from room to room. Mrs. Hardy would be up there now herself, but her knees were not what they used to be, and so the girl was exploring on her own. She really was just a girl. She'd turned nineteen only the week before. The couple had signed the marriage contract on her birthday, a happy little tidbit that caused Mrs. Hardy to release her 1000-watt whopper of a smile, jolting wrinkles that hadn't budged since Tricky Dick's second term of office. She'd consulted the lease agreement again, pegged the young man's age at thirty-two. Funny, she thought, he didn't look like a child molester.

"I can't believe you've never had a locksmith here," the cradle-robber said. "Wouldn't cost you hardly anything at all."

The girl, Janice, came bounding down the stairs. The way she bounced made the joints in Mrs. Hardy's knees ache. Her thin yellow blouse fluttered up over her flat, tan belly, and Mrs. Hardy wondered how far along the girl was. The couple had said nothing about a child, but they didn't call them shotgun marriages for nothing. If the girl wasn't pregnant, Mrs. Hardy would eat her dirty socks.

"Oh, Dave, it's *perfect!* You got to see it. I've already got it figured out where everything's gonna go, the bed and the armoire and the dresser and everything." The girl landed at the bottom of the stairs like a cheerleader finishing an inspired bit of nonsense, her hands clasped in front of her perky, baseball-sized breasts and her smile set wide as the moon. Mrs. Hardy waited for some final flourish, a Go Team! or a high kick. None came.

"Come on," the girl said. "You've got to come see it."

"I still got a few things to do down here with Mrs. Hardy, I think,"

"You mean we can really do it? Honest? We can really live here?"

"You're already measuring out the curtains. Sounds like I ought to sign the paperwork, don't you think?"

The girl clapped her hands together, a gesture that rather made Mrs. Hardy want to stick her head in the nearest trashcan and upchuck her lunch. The girl bounded through the hall and threw her arms dramatically around the young man.

"Sounds like we have an agreement, then," Mrs. Hardy said after a moment.

The young man nodded. "I find telling her no only gets me into all kinds of trouble."

"You'll find all women are like that, I'm afraid."

The girl stepped back from the young man, leaving her arm around his waist. Her whole face beamed.

"A little celebration then," Mrs. Hardy announced. She reached into her purse and removed a dwindling packet of Lucky Strikes. She knocked the packet against her wrist, deftly removed two Luckies and extended one out to the young man.

The young man's eyes went wide, flitted over to the new bride, and then he put up his hand. "No, I don't smoke."

"Phaw! Of course you do. I know a smoker when I see one."

The beaming smile disintegrated from the girl's face. She crossed her arms over those pert little melons and wrinkled her nose. "You don't smoke," she said, as if she were correcting a child.

"I don't," the young man declared. He wagged his hand to ward off the offering. "Honest. You got me wrong. I used to, but...not anymore."

Mrs. Hardy withdrew her hand. She swiftly stuck a Lucky between her teeth and replaced the other. The packet disappeared back into the depths of her purse. Once gone, the girl's face brightened. Mrs. Hardy lit her Lucky, inhaled, and held the smoke in her lungs.

"My mistake," she said, and exhaled.

The girl seemed to give the whole proceeding a last, weighty consideration, the way a judge might survey a courtroom at the end of a particularly trying day, and then she shot away and back up the stairs. She took them two at a time. Mrs. Hardy took another drag.

"Quite the whirlwind you got there."

"You have no idea."

Mrs. Hardy thought that was unlikely.

The girl called from above them. "I already know where I'm gonna put the crib! I got it all picked out!"

Mrs. Hardy smiled. Apparently, she would not be eating her socks.

***

David decided to put his desk in the basement. There was the room upstairs that was just the right size for an office, but he knew if he put it there he'd never get any work done, what with Janice coming and going from the bedroom and the bathroom and constantly making a stir. Writing needed quiet, not bustle. Besides, Janice wanted that room for the baby. She hadn't said so directly, but he knew it just looking at her face. Down here it was quiet. Down here he could work.

He unpacked the desk in stages. He'd saved the original boxes for the desk itself, though now they were tattered and flimsy, missing flaps and sporting punctures. The rest of the boxes were full of supplies and books. Paper, pens, spiral notepads, paperclips. *The Oxford English Dictionary*, *The Elements of Style*, Robert McKee's *Story*. All the tools of the trade.

In high school, David had wanted to be a playwright. He didn't care much for Shakespeare, who was real hot shit according to his teachers, but he loved the plays of Bernard Shaw and Oscar Wilde. To this day, The Importance of Being Earnest was his favorite play. When he got out of high school, he found out no one went to the theatre anymore, and there was no money in it if you weren't on Broadway. He switched to screenwriting instead, which he liked less but it paid better. Mostly he wrote for television, though four years ago he sold a motion picture screenplay called *Overlooking Colorado*. Universal owned the rights, but they hadn't made the movie. That was the life.

When he had the desk together he opened the boxes of books. He started to stack books on the shelves, making sure the shelves held. He'd just hefted a copy of Syd Field's *Screenplay* when he found a pack of Marlboro Reds lying beneath it. Immediately he looked behind him toward the stairs, but he was all alone. The basement door was closed.

"Well looky-looky," he said, reaching down and picking up the Reds.

The old bat had been right. He was a smoker. At least, he had been once. In his freshman days at Eastern Washington University he'd sat on the railing outside the theatre building with the actors and the stage crew and they'd smoked Camels between rehearsals, passing a butt around until finally someone sucked the thing dry. By the time he was a junior (and a film major, bye-bye stage) he smoked two packs a day, biting the filters off and taking them raw. His tongue inadvertently liked the rim of his teeth, remembering the feeling.

All of that changed after Janice.

Janice didn't smoke. Didn't drink. Didn't do a lot of things. At first, David found this quaintly attractive. It was like waking up in the middle of that Billy Joel song, the one that went: *Come out Virginia, don't let me wait, you Catholic girls start much too late.* In the first months of their relationship, when Janice was still just seventeen, he'd thought it would only be a matter of time before he had her laughing with sinners instead of crying with saints. But life was a funny thing, wasn't it? When he thought about it now, he realized he was the one who had given everything up. Drinking. Smoking. All the vices.

Well, almost.

David picked up the pack of Reds. There were still three partially crushed cigarettes in the pack. He fingered one out. Rifling through his supplies box, he unearthed a packet of matches. He tore one off, but just before lighting it he stopped. If he lit up down here Janice would only come down later and smell the smoke. With the washer and dryer down here, there was no way around it. He was ready to crush the match in his hand when he spied the window.

It was one of those old fashioned jobs, the small ones with four panes of glass that popped upward and swung out. David pushed it open and set the latch. The window stayed.

Perfect.

He returned to the desk, his hand reaching for the Reds. Suddenly he had a better idea. He grabbed the edge of the desk and began to drag it across the room until he situated it underneath the little window. The maneuver created an awful screeching noise of wood on concrete, and after he waited and listened for Janice. He heard nothing. He hoisted up the chair and set it in front of the desk. Then he collapsed into it and kicked his feet up onto the desk. He fingered free a Red and struck the match. Biting off the butt, he stuck in the Red in his mouth, lit it, and sucked in the smoke. Instantly, he remembered the feeling of sitting there on that theatre railing all those years ago. He blew out the smoke, watched it drift up, up, and then swirl out the open window.

"Little slice of paradise," he said. "Everything in its place."

He liked his new work room already.

***

The problem was that every time she opened her mouth she found herself talking about the color of the walls in the baby's room or where to put the baby's crib or what kind of pictures to hang on the baby's walls. She caught herself doing this and each time she tried to turn the conversation to something else, searching for some elegant, smooth, transition that wouldn't set off any alarms. Surely by now the way she went on and on he'd started to suspect. He *had* to suspect. How could he not when it was the first thing off her tongue whenever they spoke, as if she were trying to alter reality by drowning it in a deluge of babble.

"Whatever you want, honey," he kept saying. "Paint the walls whatever color your heart desires."

Staring at the walls now, currently an eggshell white that put her in the mind of an unfriendly medical facility, she wondered how long she could continue the charade. Could she keep up like this for another few weeks, another month? How long? How long until the lie became too obvious too ignore?

Little while longer honey and you won't have to worry. Little while longer and it won't be a lie at all.

Which was the same thing she'd thought two months ago. A good idea at the time, or at least it had seemed so. Now she saw it clearly for what it was: an act of desperation.

Janice popped the lid off the paint can with the end of a screwdriver. Robin's egg blue. A nearly neutral color, appropriate for either a boy or a girl, but certainly suggestive of a more masculine persuasion. A gentle kind of masculine, the color found on the walls of a boy who spends his hours caught in romantic daydreams. A pleasant boy. A boy who made his mother proud. She'd given the color quite a bit of consideration. Given that she wasn't pregnant at all, she hardly saw how it mattered.

She dipped the brush into the mild blue and pulled it back out, letting the thick ropes of paint drip back into the can. Then she smoothed off the excess and smeared the paint on the wall in a long thick streak. The blue glistened wetly atop the ugly white.

It really had seemed like a fine idea.

"You're what?" David had said.

They'd been sitting in David's Chrysler 300M in the parking lot of the baseball fields on the edge of town. It was dark, already past eleven and a school night. Janice had a test in the morning and she wasn't ready for it, had planned on studying that night, but instead had found herself thinking of April Williams who served coffee at the Vogue and the way she flirted with David whenever they were there. Even more on her mind was the way David flirted back. Casually, flippantly, laced with subtle innuendo, but paired with the slow, not-so-subtle walks his eyes took over April's lanky, slender body. April was just a few years younger than David, the kind of sexy, smart older woman men hounded after. The idea of David cheating on her had rarely entered Janice's mind, a distant thought, like an asteroid with a wide ranging orbit. Lately though David seemed distant himself, almost moody, or, worse, uninterested. His end of their conversations seemed to trail off, fizzing out like stale firecrackers that didn't explode. And in Janice's mind, thoughts of April Williams began to loom.

"I'm pregnant," she said again. She stared off into the darkness of the empty ballfields. On the far side sat the broken, ramshackle dugout, huddled in the shadows.

"You can't be. We've always been safe. We've always used protection."

"Those things aren't one-hundred percent."

"They're like ninety-nine."

"Who cares what they are? Nothing's one-hundred and it wouldn't matter anyway. I'm still pregnant. And we broke that one, or did you forget about that?"

"You took the pills afterward. The pills always work."

"Then I don't fucking know. All I know is I am. Jesus *fuck*."

In the silence which followed she was sure he wouldn't believe her, that he would call her bluff and the truth would out and it would all be over. All of it ended on the rocky shore of a paranoid lie. A cold sweat broke out on her forearms, tingling the fine hairs there and running a silent shiver through her body that made her open the window and let in more of the warm summer air.

"If we get married would you really want to be a mother?"

Which was not at all the question she was expecting. Was, in fact, so far from it that at first she thought she'd only heard it in her head. When he repeated the question Janice turned to look at him to see if he was serious, and it wasn't the steady calm she saw there that convinced her but the barely shackled terror just beyond the calm. He meant it. He meant every word.

"Yes," she said quietly, almost a whisper.

"I mean, we wouldn't have much. Not at first really. Enough to maybe get a place, at least if you found a job and all. And I'm almost done with the screenplay, and I know this one's gonna sell big. I just know it. But it wouldn't be much. Not at first."

She told him yes, and then yes again, and finally he understood and asked her proper if she wanted to marry him. She said yes and he kissed her, and because it was still before her curfew they made love in the backseat and for the first time David didn't wear a condom and when he came inside her she held him there and prayed to God to turn her lie into truth. She would make that same prayer over and over and over in coming weeks, and she never doubted it would happen. Of course it would happen. That was how these things worked. This was life, biology, birds and bees and the Rolling Stones on the radio. It couldn't be any other way.

Except it was. Her period had come again not more than a week ago, and it had been all she could do to find excuses to not have sex with David. Excuses, she was certain, he wouldn't believe. But believe them he did, and life continued, and her prayers she discovered turned to curses. How could God do this to her? She wasn't the first girl to rope a man with a lie. It was ridiculous to find herself suddenly barren. How was *that* fair?

She wanted to tell David the truth. She wanted to, but what would that accomplish? Just what would that get her?

She jammed the brush into the bucket of paint once more and smeared more blue on the wall. She smeared until the paint was thin and even and the ugly white beneath was no more.

The truth would bring nothing but pain.

It wasn't good for anything else.

***

He listened to her in the bathroom washing out her mouth and he wondered if she would cry too. He lay on the bed, the sheets damp hanging off the edge of the bed by his hand, and he waited for the faucet to turn off. When it finally did and she didn't come out immediately from the bathroom he knew she was crying. He didn't want to be there when she came out. Not now. He didn't want to fight.

He got up from the bed and pulled on a pair of sweat pants. He was hungry. More than that, he wanted a cigarette. He'd smoked the Reds though, and he had no others. As he passed the bathroom door he thought about knocking, apologizing, but what really would he say? Sometimes it happened.

In the kitchen he opened the fridge and tried to settle between the carton of 2% milk and the carton of Minute Maid apple juice. What he really wanted was a Rolling Rock. Yet another item on Janice's long list of Don't Do Its and Can't Have Its. He settled on the milk. Shutting the fridge, he unscrewed the cap and tossed it on the counter. He carried the carton to the dining room and sat at the table in the dark.

So this was marriage.

He took a long swallow of milk and wiped his chin.

This what it all boils down to? Your wife washing her mouth out in the bathroom and drinking milk from the carton in the dark? Waiting for her to go back to sleep so you don't have to fight about it? You're gonna need a bigger carton.

He smiled at that, set the milk on the table.

There had to be more than this.

Janice hadn't always been this way. When they first met she was an actress in a high school play, all of seventeen and unused to the harshness of the stage lights, so that you most readily found her hovering in the dimness at the edge of the stage, between the light and the backstage shadows. Slender, a little pale, she read her lines too quietly, as if worried someone might rebuke her. The director was a friend, had asked David to come by and rework a couple scenes they were struggling over. David came, but what interested him more than the script was the shy, nervous girl who spoke in a whisper and rarely stepped out on stage. He worked with her on her lines, sticking around long past the scene rewrites, becoming almost a production assistant. It happened a week before opening night, as David knew it would, with the two of them finally alone in the dressing room and as he helped her from her costume he kissed her. She hesitated for only a moment before kissing him back. He undressed her first and then himself and they did it there on the pile of costumes, her first time, and after as their breathing slowed he told her how he knew from the moment he saw her, how he just knew, and that he'd never wanted anything more in his life than he wanted this.

David took another gulp of milk. He thought about he'd told her that, how he'd whispered it in her ear. How he'd believed it then.

He was raising the carton for a final sip when he saw the light under the locked door leading to the other side of the duplex. It startled him so that he jumped and the carton fell from his hand. The milk splattered on the floor. A steady glug-glug-glug sounded, the milk pouring out across the floor in a stream of white. David cursed and snatched up the milk.

He looked back at the door but it was dark. He shook his head, rubbed his eyes. He waited, certain the light would come again. Milk pooled at his feet, cold between his naked toes. The darkness remained.

He stood up and crept quietly to the door. When he got close, he turned his head and listened. He heard nothing, only the noise of the house resting in the night.

Seeing things, stud. Quite possibly it's better for all of us there's no Rock in the fridge, cause you're seeing things already and all you're drinking is 2%.

Briefly, he wondered if the milk had gone bad. He caught himself sniffing at the nearly empty carton before he realized such an idea was ridiculous.

You imagined it, Chief. All there is to it. Don't worry so much. Not like you imagined little green men or the ghost of Harry Truman. You saw a light. Not exactly heavy stuff, friend. Why don't you get a rag and clean your spill?

He got a hand towel from the kitchen and began mopping up the milk. He rung out the sopping towel in the sink and went back with a second towel to finish the job. The milk ran in a thin stream across the floor and under the door. On his hands and knees, David wiped up the milk. As the towel swiped under the door his hand brushed a small object.

What the hell.

He dropped the towel and bent down, peering under the door. Just underneath he could see the dark shape of a small object. He reached out, his fingers just touching it, and he wiggled it out from under the door.

It was a key.

A tiny, brass skeleton key.

"I'll be damned."

A sudden impulse gripped him, and before he realized what he was doing he reached out and stuck the key in the lock and turned it. A soft but distinct click filled the air. A shiver ran up David's arm and down his spine. He flicked his wrist again, locked the door, and withdrew the key. He picked up the towel and stood up.

All around him the house was silent.

He left the towel on the counter. The key he took with him.

In the bedroom, Janice was fast asleep. David lay down, his back next to her. The key firmly in his hand, he tried to get some sleep.

***

She made up some lousy excuse in the morning to visit her sister, David only half-listening because he knew it wasn't true. He nodded his head and told her to drive safe and it was only when she was finally gone that he allowed himself to be angry. It was always how she handled things, running away to her sister instead of staying and working it out. What was worse (in fact, what really bothered him most) was she no doubt spilled every detail of their life to that bitch. If he wanted his private life strung up for the world to see, he'd hang a sign.

He took as shower, hoping to wash away both his anger and the minor-key headache that was brewing at the back of his mind. The shower accomplished neither, and when he was dressing he reached into his pants pocket and found the key. Immediately, he had an idea.

Let the little prude go. Let her stay away all night. A little freedom is just what a man needs.

He found a pair of old tennis shoes and pulled them on. Janice had taken the car, but there was a mini-mart a few miles down the road. He could walk there and back in an hour.

It was a warm day, troubled with only the slightest of breezes. David walked briskly, the sun on his face. He kept one hand in his pocket, the key between his sweaty fingers.

At the mini-mart he bought a packet of Reds, thought better of it, bought a second pack. He snagged two half-racks of Rolling Rock. He smiled at the clerk, a young girl who raised her eyebrows at his meager pile of sins and then glanced out at the morning sunshine.

"Getting an early start," she said with a grin, nothing but mischief in her eyes.

"Tell your boss you're sick and need the day off," David said. "Then you can find out."

Her grin grew wide, and she held up her hand with the back of it to him, her fingers dancing and he saw her engagement ring.

"I'm afraid the boss knows where I live," she said.

He carried the half-racks one in each hand and so he couldn't burn a red until he got home. He entertained a gruesome vision of returning to discover the Chrysler once again in the driveway, Janice on the porch, and his mid-morning party come to an end before it even got off the ground. It wasn't the idea of Janice discovering him that churned his stomach, but the thought that all of this might be in vain, that the Rocks in his hands might never be cracked, that the Reds in his back pockets might never be lit. The idea made him shiver.

The driveway was empty. He smiled. Life was good after all.

He set the beer on the porch and wiped the sweat off his forehead. If he'd calculated correctly, the whole trip was near six miles. A decent amount of exertion, certainly worthy of a little reward.

He was about to break open a Rock when he was struck with a new idea. He turned it over in his mind, found it agreeable. He lifted the half-racks and went into the house.

At the door he took the key from his pocket. He inserted it into the lock and turned. The soft click of the tumbler again filled his ears.

"Open sesame," he said.

The door to the other side of the house opened slowly, drifting noiselessly on its hinges. David pulled it open and stared through the door to the other side. Directly across was a hallway like his own. He picked up the beer and stepped through.

The other side of the house was a replica of his own, only in reverse. Glancing left he saw the dining room and kitchen, only here instead of extending left they extended right. Turning in the other direction, he saw the living room open off the end of the hall. The floors and walls were the same lightly tanned wood that looked more expensive than it actually was. On the walls were lonely, empty nails and the vague outlines of picture frames lingering in the dust.

He entered the living room.

"You're kidding me," he said softly.

The living room wasn't empty. In the space by the window sat an old leather rocking chair. In his own living room Janice had placed a bookshelf there, but seeing this rocking chair David suddenly understood why the bookshelf struck him as wrong. The chair faced the wall opposite the front door, and though there was nothing along that wall David saw it was perfect for an entertainment center. The chair would face the television.

"Just how I would have done it," he said.

There was space between the chair and the wall for a coffee table and room beside for a small stand and a lamp. He could see where it would all go, how it would all be, and it took him a minute before he realized that what he was envisioning was a slightly modified version of his parent's living room when he was a boy. He remembered his father in his own rocking chair, very similar to the one here, chain smoking hand-rolled Topps and watching reruns of *Rio Bravo* in his faded jeans and thick, yellowed socks. He remembered discarded plates of half-finished spaghetti cooling on the side stand and the steady accumulation of brown Budweiser bottles standing herky-jerky in a line along the floor. He hadn't thought of the old man in years. He was only just out of high school when the old man's heart gave out crossing Paterson Street downtown. A woman who saw it all happen told David later his father had been fumbling with his Topps when the attack hit him, and he spilled all his carefully rolled joints onto the street when he fell. When she got to his side he kept telling her to pick them up, don't let them scatter. David didn't cry at the funeral, and not because he was trying to hold it together but because he felt nothing, nothing at all, and later that night he got drunk and thought maybe there was something wrong with him, something decent inside him broken, but later he thought no, there was nothing wrong with him at all, his old man was shit and even though it was a sad story it was a common one, so fuck it.

In retrospect, the only thing his old man had ever done right was that living room. On that, they could agree.

David approached the chair. He ran his finger along the leather and pulled it away with a second surprise. No dust.

He sat down. The chair was soft but firm at the spine, with spacious cushions for his arms and a deep rest for his head. He gave a slight kick and the chair rocked him.

Babe in a manger. All we need now is a little TV. And a table for the beer. Speaking of which.

Rocking lightly, he reached for a Rock.

And a cigarette.

***

"What the hell do you expect?"

These, the first words out of her sister's mouth when she's done telling her story. If she'd come for sympathy, she wasn't getting it here. Her sister, Anna, older by nine years and married now for the last eight, had a lot of fine ideas about the male of the species. And she was perfectly willing to share them.

"Exactly what did you think? You'd get hitched and only have to spread your legs twice a month? Babe, you married a *man*. They want it all the time, and if you're tired or bleeding or dying of pneumonia it don't make no difference to them. They think it makes it dirtier, and if there's one thing men like it's dirt."

Saying all this on her back porch with her five children running through a sprinkler in the yard. The oldest child, Lane, seven years old, well within hearing distance, but preoccupied with digging his wet underwear out of his ass. The whicka-whicka-

whicka of the sprinkler sounding in Janice's ears, like muffled chuckling.

"That's *not* what I thought. I didn't say that. It's just that sometimes when we..."

"When you fuck."

"When we *make love*..."

And Anna rolling her eyes again.

She started over, trying to tell it so Anna could understand, so she could understand *David*. Telling again how he was the first man to ever take any interest in her, the way he had worked with her on her lines for the school play when the director had all but given up on her, how patient he'd been, all the hours reading through scenes. And after the play, how he would pick her up in the mornings and take her for coffee before school and the way he'd take her coffee when it was too hot and stir it and blow on it until it cooled. How they'd drive to the river Saturday afternoons and swim under the Falls Bridge and some days just lay in the sun on the grass and hold each other and feel each other breathe. The way he taught her things, like how to watch an audience during a movie, how the audience's reaction was always pure and never lied and that was how you knew if your screenplay worked or not. But most of all she tried to tell how he asked her to marry him, how when there were so many other things he could have said the words that came out were words of love.

"Right," Anna said. "Then you got married and now you find out he likes to smoke and drink and he farts in bed and at least once a week he wants you to get down on your knees and play How Many Licks Does It Take. Welcome to Earth, Jan."

"I don't think you understand."

"No, I understand plenty. I understand it more than you do, believe me."

Anna waved her hand at the kids who were still twirling through the sprinkler. Having decided he could not give his mission its proper attention with his clothes still on, Lane had dispensed with his shorts, flinging them in a wet heap under the sprinkler, and now dug at his naked cheeks with renewed vigor. The twin girls, thankfully still clothed, played an altered version of paddy-cake at the outer confines of the sprinkler's reach. The other two siblings, a boy and a girl, ran in ever-changing orbits about the sprinkler, laughing, howling, their arms flailing toward the sky.

"But you love your children."

"As the Sage of Nutbush once said, what's love got to do with it?"

Janice leaned back onto the porch, spreading her arms behind her head. She gazed up at the bright blue sky and traced a wispy cloud drifting all alone.

"I don't know," Janice said. "I just don't think that love is all that, you know? That when people love each other it's for who they are and what they are, and they don't make each other do things that they don't want to do. And when you love someone, you forgive them? Right? Doesn't it say all that somewhere, in a book or something?"

"Sometimes, hon, love is a quickie on the bathroom counter before work."

Janice closed her eyes. "I don't believe that."

"No, of course you don't. Look at you. All of nineteen. Christ, what I wouldn't give. You know the last time I wore a two-piece? Before Lane was born. That's when. Sure, you're all stretched out right now, thin legs and narrow hips and firm breasts, but it don't stay that way. That's what I'm trying to tell you, Jan. What you got right now ain't gonna last forever, and when it's gone what the hell you gonna have to keep old Dave at home? Nineteen. Jesus. Your marriage ain't being written by some three-hundred pound virgin working for Harlequin paperback. The sooner you figure that out the better."

Anna stood to holler at Lane, telling him to stop pulling his sister's hair, having to say it twice and put some real edge into her voice. When she sat back down she looked at Janice with eyes as narrow as daggers.

"He still hit you?"

"That was one time."

"One time means it'll happen again. Trust me, Jan. You either marry a hitter or you don't, ain't no other way around it. So."

"So what?"

"So whaddaya think, so? Does he still hit you?"

Janice huffed. "He has a temper, that's all. Sometimes I don't know when to keep my mouth shut. He doesn't mean anything by it."

"Jesus, honey. Really? That old routine?"

Janice frowned as if she were suddenly smelling something burning in an oven. For a while they were silent, watching the children and listening to the noise of the sprinkler.

"Just what is it I'm doing wrong? It's not like I tell him no."

"It's not *all* sex. You ever cook for him?"

Janice rolled her eyes. "You know I can't cook."

"Exactly. And you don't ever try. Take some advice from your big sister. Learn the tricks now. Learn them before he starts thinking about what he can get somewhere else and if it might be better than what he's got at home."

"I see. The recipe to a successful marriage is to be a whore and a cook."

"Or don't listen to me. Whine and cry about it. Maybe he'll still be around ten years from now to dry those self-centered tears."

Lane came racing across the lawn. He clamored up the porch steps and threw himself giggling onto Janice's belly. Janice grabbed him and started tickling the boy until he shrieked. Then she swung him around, lightly swatted his naked butt and sent him back into the yard.

"Why can't they just stay that age?" Janice said.

Anna shook her head. "Honey, they do. Don't you know that by now?"

***

All David could think later was that he'd given her the damn recipe. He'd written it out for her even, copied it in plain English and readable script. There was no chance of misreading it, he'd made sure of that, and he'd double checked it himself to make sure he hadn't missed any steps. And so there it was. What more was there really? He'd given her the damn recipe.

The way it happened Janice came home the next day from her sister's and wanted to cook a fancy dinner. Whatever her and her sister talked about made some big impact, because she came back all fluttery and smiling and right away David knew something was up. She hardly said anything, kissed him on the mouth and let the feel of her body linger against him, and then she was off to the kitchen. He'd left all the empties on the other side of the house, and though he'd showered he was sure she'd smell the smoke on him. He could still smell it. But if she smelled anything she didn't say, and all he heard from the kitchen was the heavy thump of the recipe book coming down from the cupboard and landing on the counter.

He decided to let her be. If she wanted to talk, she'd find him. He went to the basement to work.

When she came down half an hour later, she held in her hand one of the recipes from the book. He could tell by the crumpled and worn lined paper that it was one of his mother's recipes. Almost all the recipes in the book belonged to his mother, one of the few of her possessions he'd kept after her death.

"I want to make it, but I can't read all of it. These lines here and, well, the whole last part. Some individual words."

His mother's handwriting was notoriously difficult to read.

"Why do you want to cook it?"

"Isn't it your favorite? I thought the spaghetti was your favorite."

"It is. Why do you want to cook it?"

"For you. For us. For...I don't know." Janice put her hands on her hips. She glanced around the basement and for a moment David thought she was seeing it for the very first time. Her eyes worked slowly over the arrangement of his desk and the piles of paper in the wire basket. Not suspiciously or even with particular interest, but simply as if she'd never really noticed any of it until now. "Because you're always down here and I'm always up in the baby's room and we never have a real meal together. Because we haven't once eaten at the table and this is our *house* for Christ sakes. Isn't that why you buy a house? To have meals in a dining room instead of in front of the TV? I want to cook for you, Dave. I want to be your wife."

"You are my wife."

"Then let me cook my husband his favorite meal."

So he copied the recipe for her, taking his time, double checking, making sure he'd written everything clearly and plainly and that there could be no question left anywhere. When he was done he called up to her and she came down the stairs like a young girl traipsing into Christmas morning. He was ready to hand it to her when he stopped and said:

"You sure you want to do this? I mean, I know cooking isn't your thing."

"Give it to me."

"I don't expect you to or anything. I don't mind ordering pizza or fixing Campbell's soup, you know. It doesn't matter to me."

"The recipe." She held out her hand.

"I just want you to be sure, that's all."

He gave it to her.

"Thank you."

"You're gonna get my hopes up."

Janice ascended to the kitchen, reading the newly copied recipe on her way. At the top of the sheet were the ingredients, and she immediately made a mental list of what she needed from the store. She went straight to the key rack, took the keys and headed for the car. When she returned she dumped all the ingredients onto the counter, a raucous assortment of fresh tomatoes, hamburger, cilantro, onions, a pound of sausage, garlic, cans of tomato sauce and paste, fresh basil. Staring at the scattered pile she felt a sort of elation. Right now these were only ingredients. In a few hours they would be a meal.

At first the work on the screenplay went quickly, words nearly leaping from his forehead onto the page. Then, two things seemed to happen at once, like two cars traveling in opposite directions merging in a slow moving wreck. First, the flow of words slowed. Second, as they did, David noticed the smell of simmering garlic which had drifted down the stairs. His stomach gave the tiniest of rumbles. The smell of garlic grew stronger, and the words slowed and slowed.

The recipe called first for simmering garlic, followed by adding the onions. The garlic was to be chopped finely, the onions roughly. Janice didn't understand either term, but she figured such distinctions could hardly be all that important. The recipe called for simmering in olive oil, though it said nothing on the subject of how much olive oil. Janice guessed. Instead of feeling lost, she felt relaxed, freed even. They said cooking was an art, didn't they? Then surely the art lay in making such decisions. Surely it called for such on-the-spot variations. Already it smelled fine.

By the time he began to smell the tomato sauce cooking the words had almost stopped entirely.

They came in a lackadaisical trickle, the way water leaks unevenly from a broken faucet. David closed his eyes, his pen tapping mindlessly at the edge of the page. The deep, rich aroma wafted through the basement, slowly filling up the room and filling up David's mind. Soon, the words simply stopped.

The longer she cooked, the more "artistic" decisions there were to make. Pinch of this. Dash of that. Spice to taste. Cook until done. With each step, Janice improvised. It went smoothly in the beginning, and her confidence built steadily. However, after a while she found herself trying to do many things at once. Like a general surveying too many scattered regiments, she nervously fingered her battle plan, but the recipe said nothing about how to execute three maneuvers simultaneously, and it made no mention of a chef's assistant. Ever so slowly, her confidence began to crack.

When the words would no longer come, David dropped the pen and leaned back in his chair and let his mind wander. Naturally, it wandered down the long corridor or his memory and right on into his mother's kitchen. He recalled the days when he came in from school to find her at the stove, already stirring a large pot of spaghetti sauce, and how on some days if he came home with a good grade on a project or if his mother was simply in a light-hearted mood she would spoon a meager portion of sauce onto a wooden ladle and let him lick it clean. No doubt this could not have happened more than a dozen times in all his childhood, for his mother rarely let anyone into the kitchen while she cooked, and yet it stood out in his memory with a kind of technicolor vibrancy, an old home footage reel of the mind that hadn't dimmed with age. The smell of tomatoes and the smell of garlic and onions mingled together, and a new scent joined them: roasting sausage. David's stomach grumbled.

Janice had never juggled in her life, but in watching other people juggle she had often wondered why anyone considered it all that difficult a trick. Now, in the kitchen, embroiled in a juggling act of her own, Janice understood the juggler's plight. So many balls in the air, and gravity never cutting you any slack. The pace of the cooking, instead of slowing as she had anticipated, only increased, and as it increased there was even more to do. She rushed from one task to the next, stirring and chopping, shifting and stirring, stirring and scooping. And all the while she pondered the juggler's lament: *if only I had a third arm.*

Janice had already set the table by the time David came upstairs. If the smell was strong and distracting in the basement, here it was overwhelming. It stuck in the air like thick, greasy paste. David sat at the table and waited.

"Smells incredible," David called.

Janice flitted into the dining room with a plate of garlic bread. She sat it steaming onto the table and returned to the kitchen.

"There's a lot more work to this cooking than you can imagine," she said from the kitchen.

"You did great. I can smell it. I been smelling it for the last few hours."

Janice reappeared. "I don't know that I got it right." She set down a bowl of noodles.

"Oh, I know you did. You can't fake that smell. It's just like my mother used to make."

"Well, I don't know about that. Some of the steps were a little tricky."

Dave waved his hand at her, having none of it. "I know it when I smell it."

"I hope so."

She had poured the sauce into a glass serving bowl. She brought it out, the bowl hot, steam rising. She wore a nervous smile, setting the bowl on the table, leaving her hands to hover over it as if maybe she'd made a mistake, placed the bowl in the wrong spot. David stared at the sauce, a wide, goofy grin spreading across his face.

"It's like I'm back home," he said. "Sit down."

"Wait."

She hurried back to the kitchen and returned with the two bottles of wine Anna gave them as a wedding present. A red and a white, the only two bottles they owned.

"I want it to be special," she said.

"Jesus. Are you sure?"

Janice nodded.

"Fine. The red. Give it to me before I keel over from starvation." He uncorked the bottle and poured them each a glass, his almost to the brim.

Janice finally sat down.

David served them. He helped Janice first, and then he scooped a monstrous mound of noodles onto his plate. Noodles slid off the edge, dropping limply onto the table. David paid them no mind. He ladled four heaping spoonfuls of sauce onto the noodle mountain. It ran over them in a red torrent.

"Can you eat all that?"

"No problem. This was my favorite meal in all the world growing up. In high school I could eat two plates just like this. My god, it was awesome."

He looked very much like a little boy in that moment, that goofy grin still settled on his face, as if he were in a delightful dream from which he didn't wish to wake. He grasped his fork like a mighty spear, and in a single deft, brutal motion he stabbed it into the heap of spaghetti, twirled and hoisted a hot hunk of red noodle into his mouth.

It was all wrong.

His jaw rose and fell and before it rose a second time he was gagging. The flavor, all burnt and salted and raw, assaulted him. The violence of his reaction, a swift clenching of his throat, nearly sucked the horrid mass back further into his mouth. Choking and coughing, David spat the whole wretched, sloppy chunk onto the table. It landed in a ropy mess, splatting wetly on the cloth. It lay there in a spreading stain, mangled and still steaming.

Janice gasped. Her hand flew to her mouth.

David lifted his glass of wine, swallowed three quick gulps, then swirled and swished with the fourth before spitting it back into the glass.

"What did you do?" he said.

Janice's hand drifted numbly down from her mouth.

"What the hell did you do?" David demanded.

"I followed the recipe," Janice said softly.

"You followed the..." David glared at the plate of spaghetti in front of him. He shoved it away. It clinked harshly against the wine glass, nearly tipping it. "I wrote that recipe in plain English. I wrote it clearly and plainly. Just what part didn't make any sense to you?"

"Honest, Dave...I...all I did was..."

Tears came stinging to her eyes. Her face flushed red and hot. She slapped at her eyes, trying to beat away the tears, those damned tears which always came when they were not wanted.

"Yeah, you followed the recipe alright. No doubt about that."

"Don't say it like that," Janice said.

"Like what?"

She slapped at her burning eyes. "Like I did it on purpose. Like I *ruined* it on purpose."

"Well just how in fuck would you like me to say it, Jan? How? You want me to say good job? Want me to say, oh, baby, this is the best fucking spaghetti I ever tasted in my whole god damn life? Is that what you want? Maybe take a few more bites, see if I choke on this shit? Cause that's what this is, Jan. It's shit. Complete and total shit."

Janice was heaving now, the sobs rising up through her body. She dropped her fork and launched herself up from the table. She tried to gain some control, commanded her legs to stop wobbling, her eyes to stop crying. If she could just get a grip, get a hold, she could explain...

"Oh, for Christ sakes," David said.

"You hate it," Janice sobbed.

David pushed himself back from the table. "You're a fucking child."

"You HATE IT!"

"God damn right I do. How many times did I ask you, huh? Are you sure? Are you sure you want to go and cook a big fancy dinner? And what did you say?"

"I did it for..."

"What did you fucking say, Jan?"

"I did it for..."

"Oh, I want to cook something *special*, Dave. I want to play Susie Fucking Homemaker, Dave. I

know I can do it if I just *really, really* try. Well good
fucking job, Susie. Real fine work."

Janice lurched forward and grabbed the bowl of
sauce. "I did it for YOU!" she hollered. She
snatched up the sauce and carried it to the kitchen.

"Where you think you're going?" David rose, followed her.

In the kitchen, Janice dumped the sauce into the
trashcan. It slopped in heavy clumps, thunking at
the bottom of the can. Janice took a dirty spoon
from the sink and jabbed it at the bowl, but it jerked
off the side and spun from her hand, clattering onto
the floor and jettisoning little spheres of goo onto
the floor.

"Great job. Keep it up, Susie."

She didn't reach for another spoon. Instead, she
dug the sauce out of the bowl with her hands.

"I just wanted to make a real meal," Janice cried.

"A real meal? That what you call this?" David
snorted. "The starving nigger boys in Uganda
wouldn't eat this shit. Follow the recipe. Jesus."

"I DID!"

Janice lifted the bowl and flung it on the floor. It
shattered, shards of heavy glass ricocheting through
the kitchen. Janice brought her red hands up to her
wet eyes and her legs gave way. She toppled to the
floor in a sobbing heap.

"I made it for you," she choked, tears mixing with
sauce and smearing across her cheeks like blood.

David stared at her, at the red mess and the broken glass.

He left her there to cry.

He really needed a cigarette.

***

He didn't even go up to bed. He waited outside on the porch for Janice to go upstairs and when he was sure she was asleep he went straight to the door and unlocked it with the key. He stepped through in a rush and closed the door hurriedly behind him. What he needed was just two minutes of peace. He certainly couldn't have that with Janice in the room, not after their fight, but he couldn't even have it in the living room or out on the porch. No matter where he went he could still hear her. Or he thought he could. Or it didn't matter, because he heard her in his mind. And every time he closed his eyes he saw those bloody tears on her cheeks.

Just two minutes. That's all I'm asking. Two little minutes.

He strode down the hallway to the living room.

It had changed.

David stood in the entry and after a time when he realized there was no surprise in him he knew that he'd expected this. He couldn't say how or even why, and he didn't even consciously know it until that moment, but he'd expected it.

A nightstand stood next to the rocking chair. On the stand was a lamp.

The empties he'd left behind were gone. So were the cigarette butts.

He knew the proper emotion at this moment would have been fear, but he didn't feel afraid. What he felt was closer to wonder, closer to awe. It was like watching a firework explosion and trying to imagine how they'd managed to get gunpowder to explode into the shape of a dragon. You couldn't make sense of it, even though you knew there was some logic behind it.

He collapsed into the chair. A small whoosh of air escaped beneath him. With it went all his worries. Immediately he felt his head clearing, as if a heavy fog was finally dissipating. His entire body relaxed. The sore muscles in his back, the heavy muscles in his shoulders, the tight muscles in his neck, the tired muscles in his arms and legs, all of it escaped out of him. He sank deeper into the chair.

Moments later he tried to recall why he'd come. He'd been worried about something. He'd done something wrong, something bad. It was funny, but he couldn't remember.

He closed his eyes, drifted. He didn't sleep, but hovered in that space between sleep and reason.

As he hovered he noticed something new. At first he couldn't place it, and he waited, his eyes still closed.   Then he knew.   His nose detected a new scent.

When he opened his eyes there was a hot plate of spaghetti on the stand.   A tall mountain of noodles and a heap of sauce.   Just like his mother used to make.   It smelled wonderful.   Exactly as he remembered it.

He took the plate.   There was a fork beside it.   He picked up the fork, scooped up a twirl of spaghetti, and took a bite.

Delicious.

What other word was there?   It was exactly as his mother made it all those years ago.   In all the time between then and now he had not forgotten the taste of his mother's spaghetti.   There was nothing else like it.

He took another bite.

It was perfect.   He half expected to see his mother come out from the kitchen, a bright smile on her face.   But that was silly.   His mother was dead.

He ate until he was full, and then he kept eating.   He spooned the last half dozen bites into his mouth, chewing slowly and savoring.   He belched loudly and rubbed his stomach.   His belly hurt to burst.   But what wonderful pain.

He looked down at the empty plate.   It was smeared red.

And then, because no one was looking, he licked the plate clean.

***

Monday night there was a coffee table.
On Tuesday, an entertainment stand.
By Wednesday, a flat screen television.

***

What the hell was the point of any of it? That's what she wanted to know.

Janice flung the pregnancy test into the trash. She shoved it down to the bottom with her foot, that cruel, inhuman, disgusting, back-stabbing, two-faced pregnancy test, and covered it with a wad of toilet paper so David wouldn't see it. Not satisfied, she yanked the bag out of the trash and tied it shut. Then she tossed it to the floor.

How could she still not be pregnant? How was it possible? It wasn't. It wasn't possible at all. Which meant all of this was some sick, sick joke. All of it. Her lie. This house. Their marriage.

She fell onto the toilet seat, dropped her head into her hands and cried.

A month since her failure with the spaghetti, and in all that time she figured things could only get better. Every couple had rough patches. Every husband and wife fought. She told herself not to worry. Things could only improve.

Except they hadn't. She and David hadn't fought since that night, but nothing had improved. In fact, things had gotten worse. David spent more and more time alone in the basement, away from her. At least that's where she assumed he spent his time. His absences had become increasingly lengthy and more frequent. Twice she'd woken in the night to find him missing from bed, and both nights he didn't return until just before their alarm went off. More disturbing to Janice though, was David's sudden disinterest in her physically. Up until two weeks ago, they had made love nearly every single day, save during her periods when she found excuses to keep him away. Then, two weeks ago David's sex drive suddenly evaporated. He made no advances on her, and when she reached out for him at night he merely pushed her hands away.

And now...

Her period was three days late, the first good news in a month. And she'd dared to hope.

But she wasn't pregnant. Still.

She cried and cried.

She would have to tell David. What else could she do?

It couldn't get any worse.

***

He couldn't see the Chrysler from the bathroom window, but David heard it pulling out of the driveway. He was nearly finished shaving, and though he had no idea where Janice was going his mind was not on his wife. It was contemplating what it usually contemplated these days: the other side of the door.

He'd explored nearly every room by now. None of the others were filled with anything. They were cold and empty and quiet. Cobwebs hung in their corners. Balls of dust lay on their floors.

The living room, however, continued to fill. There was a footrest now, two rugs, a plant in the corner he never had to water. The entertainment center was complete with a stereo, a collection of classic rock CD's from his youth, a stack of men's magazines, *Playboy* and *Hustler*. On the walls were old posters from the noir films he loved in college, *Double Indemnity* and that great Robert Mitchum movie *Out of the Past*. There were pictures too, in frames on the coffee table and atop the entertainment center, pictures of himself in places he'd never been, doing things he'd never done: fishing in Key West, gazing up in wonder at the Eiffel Tower, a bizarre shot he studied again and again of himself with his arm around a woman who looked strangely like Jane Russell.

The greatest addition had come last, only two weeks ago. He smiled now, thinking about it. He wiped the last of the foam from his face. With Janice gone, there was a little time. Maybe just enough.

The one room he hadn't explored was the basement. He'd stood at the door twice with the intention of going down, and each time something had stopped him. A feeling, much like the feeling that had come on him when the living room first changed. As if he knew what he'd find down there, and so he didn't need to look.

On more than one occasion, he thought he heard something below. Something moving restlessly back and forth along the stairs.

But he'd never opened the door.

Why would he? He had all he needed in the living room.

He left the bathroom in nothing but a towel. He decided there was time. Janice was no doubt going to the store and wouldn't return for half an hour or more. Plenty of time. He pulled on a pair of underwear, a clean pair of pants. It was when he reached for his belt that he realized he didn't know where he'd left the key. His breathing stopped. He tried to remember, but his mind seemed to be working very slowly as of late. He hadn't been getting much sleep.

Surely it was in his pants. He returned to the bathroom and picked his pants up from the counter. He reached into the pockets and found them empty. Again everything froze, and a thin sliver of fear pricked along his spine. He dropped the pants on the bathroom floor. They landed in the water pooling at the edge of the shower. He went back to the bedroom.

He'd worn his robe the night before. The robe with its deep pockets. He drew open the closet and snatched at the robe. He flipped it up and around and thrust his hand into each pocket. Nothing. He flapped it in the air as if to shake the key loose and then searched the pockets again. It wasn't there. He dropped it to the floor.

His shirt. Where was his shirt? There were pockets on that shirt. He never used them, but perhaps he had last night. Perhaps he'd put the key in the shirt pocket, absentminded, mistakenly—it had to be there. Had to be—

Where was the god damned shirt?

He heaved the lid off the clothes hamper and winged it across the room. It landed harmlessly in a corner. The hamper was empty. David stared, incredulous, disbelieving, as if he'd uncovered some magical creature inside instead of empty air, a tiny unicorn or a baby sphinx. How could it be empty? It wasn't possible. It just wasn't possible.

He gave a mad bark and lifted the hamper and chucked it in the same direction as the lid. The hamper smashed loudly against the wall and fell to the floor.

He was breathing heavily now, his chest rising and falling steadily. A cold sweat broke out over his body. The fear, which had been tiny and sharp at first, was spreading, threatening to turn to panic.

Breathe, Chief. Calm. It's here. You know it's here. Where else would it be? Just take it easy and look. Just look and think. Think.

But he couldn't think. Not clearly. His head swam, his thoughts sluggish, like they were rolling through sludge. He grabbed the sides of his head, slammed his eyes shut and sat on the end of the bed. Where? Where is it? Where did he put it? Where?

Wherewherewherewherewhere

His eyes popped open.

The shirt would be in the washer. Janice must have taken all the clothes down to the washer before she left. He bolted out of the room, through the narrow hall, took the stairs two at a time, down the hall, yanked open the basement door and nearly leapt to the bottom. The washer and dryer were silent. Through the clear plastic opening of the dryer David spied a heap of clothes.

Tearing open the door, he stuffed his hands inside and began pulling out the clothes. They fell at his feet in a warm pile. Socks, pants, a skirt, two blouses, a hand towel, and then, finally, his shirt. He pulled it free with two hands, stepping back from the dryer.

The pockets were empty. It wasn't possible, but they were. He checked again. Then a third time.

Jesus Mary mother of where's my fucking key!

He wadded the shirt in a ball and flung it at the wall. It sailed compactly for half the distance and then began to unravel, the sleeves pirouetting outward before halting against the wall. The shirt slumped to the floor like a defeated dream.

A glance at the contents of the tops of the washer and dryer revealed that Janice had not removed the key from his shirt. When she found items left in his clothing she put them here, and most days he could find along the washer top a small assortment of nickels and quarters, business cards, Uni-ball pens, a pack of gum. There was nothing there now.

Unless she found it...and took it with her. Unless she kept it for herself.

The idea entered his mind with the force of a small hurricane. It ripped through his brain and caused his legs to shake. The idea, the very idea...

His own wife had betrayed him. First it was the cigarettes. Then the beer. And the television and the potato chips and the ice cream and the Gallo salami and pretty soon all of his little sins had been lined up against a wall and shot. Plugged through the head by Janice, aka The Executioner of All Life's Little Pleasures. She'd taken them all, and now she'd taken the key. Taken his last and best and why? Why? What why was there? There was no why. She took because she could. Because that was what she was. She was a taker. She was his wife.

The upstairs door opened. David froze at the bottom of the stairs. His mind, still reeling, suddenly screeched to a halt. Janice was back. He heard her move through the living room, into the kitchen. His hand reached out to the railing. He gripped it, ready to vault up the stairs, but instead he squeezed. He squeezed the wooden rail until his knuckles went white and the wood dug into his palm.

He saw how it would happen. Coming up behind her as she kneeled in front of the fridge, arranging containers of Heinz 57 and I Can't Believe It's Not Butter. Where did you put the key, baby? A turn of her head, a backward glance over the shoulder stitched together with that flirty bounce of her hair and a grade-A cocktease waggle. What key? Just what little ol' key would you be talking about? Stepping in on her, kicking aside bottles of Newman's Own fat-free, gripping the top of the fridge door. I ain't playing around. Where's the god damn key? Eyes wide, her Bambi imitation, like she'd been practicing it in front of a mirror all her ever-loving life. That smile on her face, a duplicitous contradiction found only on the lips of a woman, innocent and sweet one moment, unhinged fuck-me-baby-one-more-time the next. I really don't know what key you mean. Wanting to play it that way. Leaving him no choice. And he would strange her right there on the kitchen floor amongst the Cool Whip and the Smuckers Strawberry Preserves, his fingers sinking into that pliant flesh, her head jigging up and down thwack-thwack-thwack-thwack and the popping crack of her skull on the linoleum and a fine mist of blood across the tile. Where's the key? *Thwack!* Where's the key? *Thwack!* Where's the fucking KEY! *THWACK!* What key is that, Dave? What key would you be looking for? You lose something, Davy? Maybe it's under the bed. Maybe it's buried in the backyard. Maybe I threw it in the lake on the way to the store. No? Don't believe me? You're right. It's not there. It's up my cooch, Dave. It's up my cold, dry cunt, *HIGH* up there where little stubby Davy ain't ever gonna reach.

Dave remained at the bottom of the stairs. He held the railing and felt himself swaying. His head felt light, drifting. He focused on his breathing. In and out. In and out. Slowly the lightness went away.

He heard footsteps at the top of the stairs.

"Dave? Are you down there?"

His tongue was thick in his mouth. He coughed. "What?"

"Can you come up here a moment?"

Breathe. In and out. In and out.

"I'm coming."

She wasn't alone. Her sister stood in the living room, Janice's overnight bag in her hand, a self-satisfied snarl on her face. Janice backed away as David came up the stairs.

"Lose your shirt?" Anna said.

Dave gave her a short sneer. "What's going on?"

Janice backed all the way to the living room entry. She held her hands together meekly in front of her. She looked so much like a schoolgirl that way.

"I'm going to Anna's," Janice said.

"So go. That's hardly news. You're over there as much as you're here anyway."

"She ain't coming back," Anna snapped.

David registered the words one at a time, arranging them like puzzle pieces. He took the scene in again. The overnight bag. Janice's wringing hands. Anna's smug grin. Janice's downward eyes. More pieces to the puzzle. The picture becoming clear.

"This is about the key?" David said.

Janice finally looked up. "What key?"

Like he knew she would.

"This is about you, buddy," Anna said.

Janice turned to her sister. "I can handle this."

"I'm just saying."

"Please let me do it."

Anna shrugged her shoulders. "Handle it then."

Janice turned back. "This isn't working, David. I mean, you're never around in the day and we never talk. When we do all we do is fight. And sometimes you say the cruelest things, things I never thought you could say to me. And at night...do you think I don't notice that you're gone at night?"

"I don't sleep well. You know that."

"And you don't...you don't touch me anymore."

"You never want me to."

"That's not true. Maybe not all the time, but we haven't..." She glanced at Anna. "We haven't done it in two weeks. Not even once. And you're gone every night. What am I supposed to think?"

"How about that your husband has insomnia? That I'm too tired some nights to deal with you."

Anna snorted.

"Stay out of it," David barked at her. Anna's eyes narrowed.

David stepped forward. Janice shrunk back, but her back butted up against the entry frame.

"You think I don't see what this is?" David said. "You think I'm cheating on you go ahead and say so. You got any proof? How about it? No? Yeah, I got it." His eyes on Anna now. "You put her up to this?"

"Up to what exactly?"

"I'll just bet you did. Married a few years, you know all the tricks, don't you? Quick divorce, clean and slick. I bet you can just smell the alimony. And the child support too. Let's not forget about that."

Janice, her head hanging, whispered something he couldn't hear. Anna gave a soft, short chortle. David glared at her, then back to Janice.

"What did you say?"

She spoke again, but still he couldn't hear her. He reached out and pulled her chin off her chest.

"Speak up."

"I'm not pregnant."

The lightheadedness returned savagely, filling his skull and pushing at the backside of his eyeballs. He took his hand from her chin and placed it on the wall by her head for support.

"What did you say?"

"She said she's not pregnant. Are you fucking deaf?"

Janice's head fell back on her chest.

"Is that true?"

A soft mumble.

"IS IT TRUE?"

Janice's head bobbed up and down. "Yes. Yes. Yes, it's true."

The whole world blurred. His legs felt weak. He remembered once when he was a boy and he'd swum too far away from the dock and his body had started to cramp. His muscles ached and he'd started to go under. He swallowed two cold gulps of lake water, the world going slurry and grey before his father pulled him out. It was like that now.

"You lost the baby?"

Another mumble.

"When did it happen? When did you lose the baby?"

And her head snapped up. Her eyes blazed. She stared right at him for the first time, and he saw there all her hate and anger, but also how much she really loved him.

"I was never pregnant!" she screamed. "I never was! It was a lie, okay? I only said it because you were always looking at April Williams and she was always flirting with you and what was I, some high school girl, gonna do against April Williams?"

He remembered too the feel of his father's hand thrusting through the water, grabbing him by the hair and yanking him up and out, that first gasp of air, both wonderful and terrible, like being torn from a dream.

"You lied?"

"I just wanted you to stay with me, you know?"

"It was a lie? All of it?"

"I'm sorry."

"You were never pregnant?"

"Oh, for crying out loud," Anna said. "You mean to tell me you never noticed? She's supposed to be three, four months pregnant. Look at her! Flat as can be. You telling me you didn't know?"

Janice stepped away into the living room. "I'm going, David. I packed a few things just for the night."

"We'll be back in the morning for the rest," Anna said.

"I wanted you to have some time to think," Janice said. She was starting to cry now, or she had been crying and he was only now noticing. "I really did love you."

They walked out the front door together. David didn't move. He didn't move until he heard the car

leave the driveway. His first few steps were tenta-
tive, shaky. He needed to lie down.

As he passed the key rack he stopped.

Janice had found the key after all.

She'd hung it on the rack.

***

He felt that it might be important to wait, that this
might all have been some cruel joke and if he waited
Janice would return and tell him she was sorry and
life could go back to normal. He sat in the dining
room with the key in his hand and stared at the door.
He told himself to wait. For some reason it was important.

After ten minutes had passed he could stand it no
longer. He jumped out of the chair and stabbed the
key into the lock. He twisted, listened to the tumbler
click. The door opened. He went through.

The air was lighter on the other side. He never
understood why or how this was true, but he
breathed easier over here. He shut the door behind
him, leaned against it and took two deep breaths.

*What a shitkicker day. You think you've got it all figured
out, everything on autopilot, smooth sailing friend.
Then...this shit. Like flying smack into a flock of fucking
geese. There goes engine No. 2, Dave. We're on fire. Hou-
ston, we have a problem. Sucked a long neck into an engine.
Yeah, just our luck.*

That was life.

He went to the living room. He fell into the chair with a disgusted sigh, but once there his mind began to clear. Janice drained from his mind. Anna drained from his mind. The baby that never existed, the marriage that was falling apart, the empty house as empty as his life, all of it drained and drained, dirty water swirling down a dark and gurgling pipe. If he was quiet, he might hear it go.

He didn't need her anyway, he thought. He didn't need her moping around with her hang-dog pout, didn't need her lousy cooking, didn't need her frigid lovemaking. He didn't need her and he didn't need the baby. Didn't need any of it. Not now. Not ever again. He was happy right here. He was happy on this side of the door. Over here, he had everything a man could want.

He sighed, leaned forward and took up a Rolling Rock and the remote. He cracked the Rock open, relaxed into the chair. He turned on the TV. The TV came to life, but the channel was static. He grunted. In all his time here, he'd never once found the TV on the fritz. Every channel came in bold and clear.

Huh. Bad reception, I guess. Can't get good service any-where these days.

He flipped the station. More static. Again. A blur. Again and again and again. All the channels the same, one after another, all a useless chatter of black and white. His finger jabbed at the remote, but it made no difference.

Then, suddenly, a single clear channel. He stared.

"You're shittin' me."

It was Dr. Phil.

He clicked the TV off. He took a swig of beer. It tasted wrong in his mouth, flat and stale. He swallowed with a grimace.

"What's going on here?"

He put down the beer and turned to look at Janice laying on the couch behind him. She was naked as always, her hair done up and curled the way he liked it. Her hands behind her head so that her perky breasts thrust from her chest, nickel sized nipples jutting toward the ceiling. Entirely smooth between those beautiful legs, something she'd refused to do for so long, said it made her feel like a little girl, ten years old again. However she felt about it, that smooth, bare valley really sparked his engine. He got up from the chair and went to the couch.

"The beer is flat and the TV's on the damn fritz."

Janice gazed up at him with those black eyes, pure, shiny orbs of coal, the only part of her that he couldn't get used to. He couldn't look at those eyes when he fucked her. He turned her around instead so he wouldn't have to.

"We're a family, Dave," Janice said.

"I know, baby. We're always gonna be. I love you, you know that."

"We're all a family."

He looked away from her eyes, down to her tits. "Tell me how old you are," he said, starting the game.

"Seventeen."

"Only seventeen. Not even legal."

"Not even," she repeated.

"You look old enough to me," he said.

He put his hand on that bare mound, his cock already hardening in his pants, slid his finger down that hairless slit and then in, in and up and—

She was cold inside. Cold as ice. He jerked his hand away.

"What's going on?" he said.

"We're a family, Dave. *All* of us."

"What about it?"

"Families don't leave each other. You shouldn't have let her leave."

He stared now into those black eyes and he knew. He stood up and went back to his chair. He sat down and drank stale beer, and in the quiet he could hear the insistent scratching at the basement door. The noise, he knew, had grown louder and louder each day. Some days there was only the tramping on the basement stairs. Some days there was scratching. Some days the door jerked against a non-stop pounding from below. If he turned up the TV, though, he couldn't hear it. Most days.

"Families stick together, Dave," Janice said from the couch.

"I know," he said.

"They're always there for each other. For ever and ever."

David sipped his beer. "For ever and ever."

***

Anna was supposed to come with her but Lane had woken up puking. The poor kid. He shivered and cried and threw up some more, all vomit and tears and fear, and Anna had looked at her and put up her hands. What could you do? So she showered and dressed and left by herself. She didn't mind really. It would be nice to have Anna with her, a little moral support, a little backbone, but all she was doing was packing a few things. Packing and leaving. She could do that on her own.

She drove Anna's Volkswagen. They'd left the Chrysler at the house yesterday. It was David's car after all. She stopped and bought a coffee on the way. A few shots of caffeine would steel her nerves.

When she parked the Volkswagen in the driveway she stared through the windshield at the duplex and it came to her that this was probably the last time she'd ever think of this place as home. It was a thought that should have saddened her, but at that moment she realized all she felt was relief. She didn't know if that made her a bad person or not.

The front door was unlocked. She entered quietly. She hadn't called ahead and didn't know if David was still asleep. It was early, and though he would normally be awake by now, it would not surprise her to find him passed out upstairs. Getting drunk, she knew, would have been his first impulse after what she'd told him yesterday. Getting drunk and trying to forget.

The living room was the same as she had let it, indeed, the same as when she had first arranged it. She'd never altered the arrangement. She remembered now the hour upon hour she'd spent moving and shifting the furniture, the plants, the pictures, the shelves, all the minute details which she'd believed, if arranged just so, would ensure a happy marriage. *A happy home is one where no pictures are tilting off center, isn't that right, Jan?* Everything in its place. Except some things had never been centered from the start, the parts of their marriage you couldn't even see, unstable ground all the more treacherous for being invisible. The living room now looked foreign to her, the work of another woman whose taste Janice didn't quite care for. It did not feel like home. Janice thought now that it never had.

The house was silent. She thought briefly that she might just get lucky. If David was passed out upstairs she could gather her things and go. Maybe she wouldn't have to talk to him at all. She thought about the look on his face after she'd told him the truth, the way his cheeks had sunk inward and his eyes had glassed over, like watching a small boat sinking into a shallow pond. She'd never seen him that way, so utterly devastated. She didn't want to see it again.

She crossed into the hall and saw the door to the other side of the duplex standing open.

Now that's funny. I thought it was locked.

She went to the door and turned the handle. It twisted smoothly.

But there isn't any key.

She peeked her head through the door. The other side was just like the one she'd been living in, only in reverse. She couldn't make any sense of it, this door being open. David must have found the key, but where had he found it? Where had it been hiding for twenty years?

This is about the key.

David's words, coming back to her. Was that what he said? This is about the key?

"David?" she called.

There was no answer. This side of the house was just as silent.

You've got things to do, babe. None of them includes tramping through the other side of this house.

"Dave? Are you over here?"

She stepped through the door. If David was over here, if he'd somehow found the key to this door and had come over here in a drunken stupor, he might be passed out on the floor somewhere. Even as her life in this house was coming to an end, she still found a part of her that cared for David. The thought of him passed out over here just didn't sit right with her.

"Dave? Answer me."

It was dusty over here, twenty years of stale air and stagnant domestic dreams that never came to pass. She glimpsed the bare nails on the walls, the outlines of picture frames. She moved toward the living room.

My God.

It was just like the other side, she thought.

The room was totally bare. An exact replica of the other living room, reversed, and seeing it brought a flood of memories of the day they'd moved in. She remembered the excitement in her belly watching David sign the papers, remembered shaking Mrs. Hardy's stiff, wrinkled hand, remembered the boxes coming in one at a time and piling in the empty rooms. All of it gone now. All of it over, and her memories only outlines in the dust.

"Hello, Jan."

She nearly screamed. David's voice, coming from almost right behind her. She whirled around, saw him standing in the hall. She had not heard him approach. Her heart fluttered in her chest.

"Christ, David. You scared the hell out of me."

He looked tired, worn, like he hadn't slept at all or he'd slept on a floor which hadn't treated him well. His face was haggard, still sunk with that hollow visage, his cheeks like pale, deflated hunks of dough.

"What do you want?"

"I thought you were over here. The door was open. You must have found the key."

This is about the key.

"Yeah. I'm over here a lot."

His voice was tired too, like it was an effort for him to talk, as if he were dragging his voice up from a well on a rusty chain.

"I came for the rest of my things," Janice said. David was blocking the hall, and she suddenly wanted to get back to the other side of the house and finish what she'd come to do.

"I collected them for you."

"You what?"

"Your things. I collected them."

"Did you break anything? Damnit, you better not have broken...just because we..."

She felt the anger rising in her. She was stupid to leave anything here with him. She should have taken everything yesterday. Yes, all in one load. Cut the cord quick and clean and be done with it. But she hadn't, and now there was this. She could see David collecting, as he called it, taking each and every one of her possessions and raising them above his head and bringing them crashing down on the bedroom floor. Collecting indeed. And after all that collecting? A beer, of course. A reward for all the hard work.

"Is that what you did? Break everything?"

"Why would I do that?"

"I don't know. For shits and giggles."

"Everything's fine now. It's all fine." His voice still like sludge, his lips moving slowly, as if he was struggling for the right words.

"Are you alright?"

"Fine. Wonderful. What's wrong? Don't I look happy?"

He smiled, the lumps of his cheeks sifting like gas under curdled milk. It was hideous.

"You look like hell."

The smile fell. "You want your things? I packed them. Put them in their place."

"I just want to get my stuff and go."

"Where should we go?"

"We're not going anywhere. I'm going to Anna's. I don't know about you, Dave. I really don't. And you know, I don't want to know either. I just can't take it anymore."

"We're a family, Jan."

"Not anymore."

His eyes raised up to the ceiling as if he were pondering this, as if maybe the answers to why their marriage failed were written up there in the dust.

"We're a family," he said again.

Janice sighed. "Just show me my things."

His eyes leveled, gazing at her again. "Yes. They're through the door."

She was already weary of all this, found that even this short conversation had zapped any boost the caffeine had given her. Living with David was hard. Leaving him was just as difficult.

"Show me."

She took three steps forward, toward the door to the other side of the house, trying to brush past David without touching him. As she did, he reached out and grabbed her arm.

"Get your hands off me," she growled.

"Wrong door," David said.

He reached out with free hand and pulled open the basement door.

"You put my stuff in the—"

In one swift, sharp motion David flung her down the stairs. She fell headfirst into the darkness. For a brief, startling second her mind understood what had happened, what a mistake it had been to come alone, and she thought of Anna, who would be waiting.

And then she hit the stairs. They were wooden steps just like on the other side of the house. Strong old boards. She didn't see them for the darkness. She hit the first stair with her left arm. It broke at the elbow as she tumbled. A loud *crack!* went off in her ears and a flame shot up her arm. She hit the next stair with the side of her head, jerking her neck sideways. The darkness filled with the light of a billion jumbling stars popping like exploding fireflies. She came down on the third stair with the small of her back, a pain so jolting it knocked all the air from her lungs. She vaulted forward up into the air, and she hit the final stair face first. The wood smashed through her front teeth, ragged splinters stabbing into her tongue. Blood spurted hot into her throat, poured over her chin. She gagged, trying to fill her stunned, empty lungs, and felt her shattered teeth sucked down into the back of her throat. When she came to a halt at the bottom of the stairs, everything was pain. Everything was agony.

The light came on.

David stood at the top of the stairs. He stared at her. He descended slowly, taking his time. She could not see him clearly. Her eyes pulsed with waves of blackness which threatened to shut out the light altogether. All she could see was David's blurred shadow slowly growing larger.

David stopped three stairs from the bottom. He sat down. Resting his elbows on his knees, he leaned forward, studying her.

"You ought to watch your step," he said.

Then he stood and stepped past her.

Janice gasped for air, but her throat felt thick and funny and the air would not come in the large gulps she desired. She heard David moving in the basement behind her, and then a sound she couldn't identify. A scraping sound. He was dragging something along the basement floor.

When he came back into her field of vision, she blinked. The image cleared slightly.

He was holding an axe.

She tried to shake her head. It wouldn't move.

"We're a family," David said. "And families stick together."

She started to cry.

He raised the axe.

***

Mrs. Hardy wanted to simply mail the papers, but the young man insisted she come out. He wanted to sign them and have it done with. She thought about asking Mr. Frank to do it, but then she chided herself. Even if everything they said was true, she thought, the young man had no reason to harm her. So she gathered the paperwork and drove to the duplex.

The young man was sitting on the porch. Not his porch, the other one, and right off it disturbed her. She didn't know why, and later that night when she would think about the way he sat there rocking on the wrong porch and all her mind trying to forget him, knowing she would dream of him, nightmares, and even then she couldn't say specifically what bothered her.

He was more handsome then she remembered, and this bothered her too. He didn't look like a man who would kill his wife.

"Mrs. Hardy," he said jubilantly. "Good morning! You got my papers?"

"That's why I'm here."

"And I thought you just came for the small talk. A little town gossip." He smiled.

Mrs. Hardy tried to return the gesture, and for the first time in memory she couldn't bring it off. She coughed into her hand to cover her inability. She took out the papers and handed them over with a pen.

"They're same as the others, so you know. I asked Mr. Frank about a discount, renting out both sides at once, but he wouldn't have it. He said if you want to rent both, you have to pay double. That's all there is to it."

"Mr. Frank is a fine businessman," David said. He flipped through the papers, signed in all the right places.

"Sure is a lot of space for one person," Mrs. Hardy said, the words out before she realized she was going to speak.

David stared at her thoughtfully, capping the pen. "I just tell myself that maybe someday she'll come back. You know, maybe she'll get tired of wherever she went and she'll come back and we'll be a family again. I think about that a lot. A family. Everyone needs a family. A family sticks together through thick and thin."

You'll be waiting a long time, Mrs. Hardy thought, if it's anything like Carol Jackson says down at the salon. A bash to the head and drop her in the river. Course, they combed that river. Twice. But there's a swift current. And other places to hide what you don't want no one to find.

"That all of them?" he asked.

She looked over the paperwork. "Got them all," she said.

"Say, you wouldn't happen to have any of those Luckies still would you? I'm all out."

Mrs. Hardy folded the papers and placed them in her purse. She wanted to tell him no, she'd smoked her last. No, she'd quit. No, she'd never smoked in her whole life. Who was he to ask?

"I thought you didn't smoke."

"Yes, well...old habits and all that."

Reluctantly, she took out her pack of Luckies, drew one out and handed it to him. Briefly, for only a fraction of a second, their fingers touched.

The key the key the key

He had his own lighter. He lit the Lucky and took a long, languorous drag.

Mrs. Hardy felt sick.

"You know," he said. "It's like my own slice of paradise."

Echo

WE'VE NEVER MET, you and I, or maybe we have and you've forgotten who I am. Maybe we were close once, and I slept over at your house on summer evenings, ate hunks of pie your mother cooked from fresh apples, perhaps we even sliced our fingers and mashed the blood together and swore oaths to each other. But you've forgotten all this.

It's okay. Really. I forgive you.

I must ask you a favor, though, dear reader who no longer remembers my name or my history or the things we did together. Stop now, whatever you are doing, and share this page.

Please.

Not ten minutes from now and certainly not once you've come to the end of this post. Because the simple truth is that what you're reading, my last testament of sorts, may not exist ten minutes from now.

So please.

Pause, click share, and send this to everyone you know. Copy it, email it, follow it on your Facebook.

It's important. Critical. Life and death, my friend. Mine, certainly, and maybe yours in the not too distant future. All I ask is that you spread the word that I once lived and breathed, that I am not a figment of your imagination, that my story, wild and incomprehensible that it may be, truly happened.

Because it did. And it may happen to you.

My name was—is—Jonathan Echo Maywood. I am eighteen years old. I lived, for a time, at 16625 E Nixon Avenue in the town of Lake Chelan, Washington. I was real. I existed.

Don't forget me.

***

All of this began, as far as I can tell, on the Wednesday after Lisa's homecoming party. It may have begun long before, but I never noticed it until then.

Lisa's parents were what most teenagers considered cool: moderately young and moderately wealthy, attractive, and often inebriated. Lisa's father had once played football for Notre Dame, and he considered the homecoming game a fine excuse for throwing a bash, as he liked to call it. It was a two-story affair. Adults upstairs passing around cabernet sauvignon and hand-crafted beer, Dusty Springfield on the stereo, wives in the kitchen chattering over mini-franks and water chestnuts wrapped in turkey bacon. Downstairs were us kids, fully stocked with our own supply of Coors Light and bottles of Hennessey that we passed around, taking slow swallows and nodding approvingly, as if we'd spent all the formative years of our lives judging fine liquor. Eminem and Snoop blared from the surround sound. Every half hour or so someone would flip it over to Journey, and all the girls would squeal and rise up like a flash mob and dance, bobbing it out to the soundtrack of their small town hearts, and the guys would lean back and sip their beers and watch.

This was the start of our junior year. We'd seen a dozen parties like this one, and there was nothing particularly memorable about it, save one event. Sometime after her fourth or fifth shot of Hennessey, Ariel leapt up from the couch and bolted for the bathroom. Even this was unremarkable, but when she burst through the bathroom door I happened to be on the pot. She took one look at me, pants around my ankles, one hand on the toilet paper, and then Ariel yanked the shower curtain aside and spewed into the empty bathtub.

Which was, of course, the moment everyone else spilled through the open door. Mikey lead the pack, his iPhone already held out like a shiv he intended to shank someone with. I held up my hands.

"Mikey, man, don't."

But it was too late. He snapped half a dozen photos before I could even look away.

Ariel wretched again, and the crowd alternately laughed and held their hands over their noses. Mikey shook his head slowly, staring at his phone.

"This is some real Ansel Adams shit right here," he said.

"Don't post those, Mikey," I said. "Come on man. Don't be a hater."

He was already slipping back into the crowd, though, and I knew those pics would be on Facebook before I'd even wiped my ass.

For the next four days I endured a relentless torrent of juvenile ribbing, both online and in the hallways and classrooms of Lake Chelan High. In the pics you could only see Ariel bent over the side of the tub, her head mostly out of sight behind the shower curtain, the smooth curve of her ass in black yoga pants. But the bathroom light lit me up like a ray of sunshine cutting through a dark cloud. There I was in all my glory, one hand splayed in the air, my mouth open in a wide O, shock and a plea for mercy there in my eyes. Pants around my ankles, skinny legs and knobby knees, the angle just right so you could actually detect a dark patch of pubic hair. A picture worth a thousand words, nine-hundred of which were Humiliation.

Then, on Wednesday, after finishing two pages of pre-calculus and reading three chapters of *Lord of the Flies*, I pulled my Facebook up on my laptop and found that the pictures were gone.

I sent Mikey a text.

Thnx for taking down the pics bro.

WTF u talkin bout?

The pics from Lisa's party.

???

You know what pics. Me & Ariel.

Whatever dude.

To be honest, I didn't give it much thought. I figured Mikey was stoned or in the middle of a *Halo* tournament, his mind distracted. Or maybe he was simply uncomfortable with discovering he could be a decent human being. It didn't matter.

I text Ariel to let her know. She hadn't been taking as much shit as I was, but there'd been a number of cracks about her ass and the noticeable lack of panties her yoga pants revealed.

M took down the pics. Thought u should know.

What pics?

W/me & u at Lisa's.

Which party?

Homecoming. Friday night.

This homecoming?

What was with people? Of course this homecoming. What other homecoming did she think I was talking about?

Yes, THIS homecoming. The pics in the BATH-ROOM.

There was a long pause on Ariel's end, and my phone went black. When it buzzed a few minutes later, I snatched it up, punching in my four-digit passcode.

What I read sent my world off-kilter.

Eko, you weren't there.

***

Most people thought I was joking.

A typical interaction looked something like this:

Me, striding down the school hallway, pausing at a locker. Classmate and fellow attendee of Lisa's party, shutting their locker, hitching an overloaded backpack higher on their shoulder.

Me: Great party at Lisa's. Man, her parents really know how to let loose.

Classmate: Wish my parents were like that. Someone shoved a stick up my dad's ass before I was born. You couldn't dislodge that thing with a backhoe and ten pounds of C4.

Me: Yeah, mine too. You believe that Ariel still can't hold her liquor? You'd think she'd learn her lesson, you know?

Classmate, puzzled: She seemed alright to me.

Me: Well, sure, right until she threw up in Lisa's bathtub.

Classmate, bewildered and backing away: We talking about the same party?

Me: Course we are. I was there, man. You don't remember that?

Classmate, awkwardly grinning: You're shitting me, right? What is this, like some kind of hidden camera bullshit? You weren't there, Echo. I was there. We all missed you, buddy. You should come to the next one, though. I hear Lisa's dad wants to do another party for prom. Gonna be bitchin.

Me: starting to open my mouth.

Classmate: hurrying away.

After the fifth time, I gave up. Nobody remembered me being at the party. Nobody remembered Ariel upchucking into Lisa's bathtub either. Like it never happened.

But it did.

It's funny what you learn to live with. I spent two weeks trying to convince Ariel and Mikey and Lisa and Julie that I was at that party, but every time I brought it up what I got in return were rolled eyes, heavy sighs, and pitying stares, like I was some poor child caught with stolen goods who refused to admit the deed.

So I gave up.

I told myself I'd simply remembered things wrong. I told myself I'd had a particularly vivid dream, brought on perhaps by a potent mixture of Absolut vodka and cannabis, and my dream had wandered into my reality like a dog straying through a hole in a rickety fence, nothing more. Because what else was there?

What other explanation made sense?

I gave up, and life continued on its merry way. Quizzes followed homework which was assigned after FBLA meetings which came before tennis practice.   Ever so slowly, the mundane buried the impossible.

I truly thought it was over.

Boy was I wrong.

***

"But Mr. Loucks, I *did* the assignment."

"Then I should see your account linked to mine, at the very least an invite to link to mine. And I don't see either. It's as simple as that, Echo."

Mr. Loucks leaned back in his chair. The bearings squeaked.

"I linked it to yours," I said. "I swear I did."

"I'm afraid not."

"There's got to be a problem with my LinkedIn."

"Show me your account," Mr. Loucks said. "If it's just my account you haven't linked to, then I can still give you most of the points."

Mr. Loucks pushed his keyboard across his desk. I bent forward and scrolled back to the LinkedIn log-in screen. Mr. Loucks waited patiently, hands folded in his lap.

Account name/password not found.

"Damnit," I said. "I must have typed it in wrong."

I entered my account information again, slowly this time, watching every stroke.

Account name/password not found.

"A different name, perhaps?" Mr. Loucks said, still giving me the benefit of the doubt.

I tried two other name and password combinations. I knew they were both wrong, old pairings I'd used in middle school and abandoned long ago. I knew the account name and password. I wasn't typing anything in wrong. It was the system. It was LinkedIn. It was the internet.

Mr. Loucks is a pretty good guy. He looked like he might have once had a cameo in *Revenge of the Nerds*, and on Fridays he liked to tell stories about wild, drunken shenanigans he engaged in during college, the kind of stories adults believe endear them to teenagers but somehow only result in a queasy, awkward rumbling in the bowels. He'd never married, which was unfortunate, because he left home each morning wearing wrinkled short-sleeved dress shirts with unmatched ties and flip-flops. Still, he was a good teacher, fair and patient. He let me call my father, a sort of last ditch effort to prove I hadn't blown off this assignment for the last two weeks.

"Echo, that you son? One of your psycho classmates isn't shooting up the school is he?"

This was Dad's idea of a joke.

"Dad, listen, what's your LinkedIn log-in information? I can't get mine to work, and I have to show

Mr. Loucks that I created an account and did the assignment."

"So you're gonna show him mine?"

"No. I can get to my account through yours."

"How's that?"

"Because we set mine up together, remember? When you helped me create my account, you linked to yours first thing. So if I'm on yours, I can get back to mine. I'll be in your links."

There was a pause, the sound of Dad shuffling papers, a woman's voice asking him a question he must have answered with his hand over the phone.

"Echo, are you sure it was LinkedIn we set up together? I remember doing your Gmail account."

"Dad, that was sixth grade."

"Yeah, you're right. Hell, whatever. Don't get old, son. That's my fatherly advice to you. Don't get old. You just forget everything. I'd forget my...holy shit, who am I talking to?"

"Funny, Dad."

"Wait, I have a son?"

"Ha-ha. Your log-in and password?"

He gave them to me, told me he loved me, and reminded me to be home for dinner.

"Got it?" Mr. Loucks asked.

I nodded. I entered Dad's information and pulled up his account.

Two-hundred and fifty-seven links.

But not to me.

"Sorry, Echo," Mr. Loucks said. "I'm gonna have to give you a zero."

***

Julie and I had only been dating for three months. We'd been friends, though, since sixth grade, hung out at parties, met up at Lakeview Drive-In for fries and milkshakes in the summer. She'd invited me out on her dad's boat half a dozen times over the years, and in eighth grade she came camping with my family up at Dry Lake. I liked the way she looked at you crosswise, as if uncertain to take you seriously or punch you in the shoulder. She was the smartest girl I knew, and one of the prettiest in our class. She told me I was different from other guys, that I actually listened to her instead of just nodding occasionally while staring at her breasts. I took this as a compliment, although it seemed like a rather low bar.

We started dating after Braydon's Christmas party. Braydon's parents owned a cabin up Boyd Road, an isolated three-room shack with a fireplace and various animal heads on the walls that creeped-out the girls and put the guys in in the mood to talk guns, hunting, death. Braydon threw a Christmas party every year, which meant he invited a bunch of us up to the cabin a few days after Christmas to get drunk and play *Halo 2* or *Grand Theft Auto* until the girls got fed up and demanded we all go outside and build a snowman. Julie and I ended up on the living room floor in musty sleeping bags, talking into the night as the fire slowly died. That was all we did, talk, but when the sun poked between the shades to find us still awake and chattering, I think we both believed there might be more to our friendship than we'd thought. We agreed to give it a try.

I won't say that we were in love. But we spent a good deal of time together those three months. I learned a lot about Julie, like that she loved Nicholas Sparks movies but thought his books were poorly written; she preferred Colbert over Jon Stewart; donuts were the one vice she allowed in her otherwise sterling diet, but only maple bars and only on Tuesdays. We had sex seven times, always at Julie's and only on nights when her mom pulled a double shift in the ER (sorry Mrs. Ellis). We laughed a lot, and the only time we ever fought was over a test Julie felt I should have studied harder for.

I didn't have the nerve to tell her the test had been online, that I'd done it, that it got swallowed up like everything else.

Like any modern couple, we documented our relationship online. Our Facebook statuses read: In a Relationship. We created photo albums strictly devoted to us and our adventures. We took selfies together, hurried and at careening angles. When we went to a movie or spent a weekend afternoon on the banks of the Columbia River, we tweeted our position in the world, our state of mind, our emotional gradient for all to see. It's only now that I wonder if we'd kept it all private, if we'd never posted any of it, not one single picture, not one random comment, would it have all been safe? Would whatever was happening to me be unable to get to her?

The first pictures to go were shots of us at the drive-in theater in Wenatchee. We'd gotten there early with enough light in the sky for half a dozen pictures on the hood of Julie's Toyota Camry. I held a bucket of popcorn like it was the Holy Grail, and Julie grinned mischievously while pretending to stick the straw from our shared cherry Coke up her nose. We'd been dating a month and were already sharing straws. It was the only movie we saw together at the drive-in theater: *Crazy Stupid Love.* They closed it down a few weeks later, one more victim of a depressed economy.

By the time the pics disappeared from my Facebook, I'd already started keeping tabs on my entire online life. Bit by bit, my digital footprint was shrinking, mostly in ways that didn't seem to matter, as long as you didn't ponder the long-term implication. Who cares much if a charge of $14.98 at Hot Topic vanishes from your bank record? Or your Getsixpackabs.com daily email alerts suddenly stop because you no longer have—and never did, according to their records—an account? The drive-in pics, however, bothered me. They were good shots of a good day, and their loss felt like coming home in the night to find the window shattered and something precious stolen.

Julie didn't miss them at all.

She didn't even know they were gone.

A month after that, she no longer recalled that we'd ever dated. My Facebook timeline was a series of gutted holes, whole weeks and months gone, whole chapters of my life torn out and discarded.

On May sixth, only a few weeks before graduation, Julie didn't remember me at all. I sat next to her that morning for senior English. She turned and gave me that sideways stare, the one that always made my heart thud half a beat faster than normal.

"Hi," she said. "I'm Julie. Are you new here?"

***

How much of your life is out there, online, in the void? How much of you exists in that digital world? How much do you have to lose?

Could it be...everything?

Birth records. Dental records. Doctor's visits.

Bank accounts. Credit histories. Job applications.

Emails. Instant messages. Texts.

Video surveillance. Voicemails. Those calls they record when you dial customer service.

Airline tickets. Concert tickets. Parking fees.

Amazon and Ebay.

Insurance. Transcripts. Taxes.

It's all there. It's your life. It's the shadow all your living and breathing casts, stretching out so far behind you that you no longer can tell what it touches back there in the distance.

How long, you think, would it take to systematically remove it all? To extract every trace you left behind, until it was like you'd never been, never were, and never would be again.

It took two weeks shy of nine months. Like a pregnancy in reverse.

***

My name is Jonathan Echo Maywood. I am eighteen years old. I was supposed to graduate from Lake Chelan High School two weeks ago, but there is no record of me ever having gone to school, not in this district, not anywhere. I am typing this blog at an internet café called Murray's Coffee House and Computers. There is a poster on the wall above me exclaiming in bold blue print: Like Us On Facebook! I cannot go home. My own mother no longer recognizes me. I know this because when I came home this morning, she took a butcher knife from a kitchen drawer and thrust it at me, screaming and threatening to call the police. She had, she claimed, no children. A quick scan of her Facebook confirms this. There are no longer any pictures of me there, no baby photos, no birthday shots of me blowing out candles, no awkward pics of the first day school. My own Facebook account no longer loads. For good measure, I looked up my birth certificate on the Chelan Hospital's online database. Nada. If you looked in through the café window just now, I wonder what you would see. Because in this world—your world, friend—I was never born, and I do not exist. Would you see a ghost?

The only evidence of me left is this blog, dear reader, whoever you are. Which is why I beg of you to share this page. Don't bookmark it. Don't add it to your favorites. Share it. Share it with as many people as you can. Because what time I have left may honestly depend on it.

To tell the truth, I haven't felt so good this last month. I thought at first I was coming down with a cold, or that all the stress was finally getting to me. But it's not a cold, and it's not stress. I feel...less substantial, if that makes any sense. Less here.

The barista has informed me that they will close in ten minutes. I have asked her if I can stay while she mops up. At first she didn't hear me.

"Oh, well," she said. "I didn't see you there."

I still have my laptop in my backpack. It's fully charged. I think it's warm enough outside that I can spend the night in the park behind Murray's. If I stay close to the back of the building, I can probably pick up the internet. I can keep typing. I just have to stay awake. It's the only chance I have really. I have to keep posting. Keep casting that shadow.

Hear she comes again. She's going to tell me now that I have to go.

No...maybe not. She's only turning out the lights. Maybe she has more to do. She's going to let me stay awhile longer. Taking pity on me. I must look pretty worn thin. Checking the door now, making sure it's locked tight.

Look, if you're following this—and I know this is a lot to ask—but can you, dear reader, stay up late with me tonight? Maybe just hit refresh every ten minutes or so, make sure this page still loads. Could you copy it and paste it into your own blog? Or even just as a file on your hard drive. The more of me there is out there the better, wherever it may be. I don't think it matters. I think what matters is just that it's there. I'm there. I'm out there in the void. Me, my life. I can be found somewhere in all those radio waves, buzzing through fiber optic lines, my life translated into a series of ones and zeros, my flesh and my blood converted into data, transferred and stored, uploaded and downloaded, tagged and posted and friended and shared. That's what matters.

That's all that matters.

So please, old friend, can you help me? Will you help me?

I don't know how much longer I can type.

I'm just so tired.

The barista is coming back. I'm going to ask her if she can log on before she leaves. If she'll share this too. She looks like someone with a lot of friends. She's looking right at me. Smiling. Like someone whose problems have all been swept away. God she's pretty. She looks like someone wh

Afterward

WHEN I WAS A BOY, my favorite show on television was *Are You Afraid of the Dark?* Which more or less tells you the kind of kid I was. I loved Halloween (still my favorite holiday), the month of October, and most of all I loved tales dark and spooky and just a little bit off-kilter.

Like a clown at midnight.

Today, as a healthy and well-adjusted adult, I find that my tastes are not all that dissimilar to those of the twelve-year-old boy I once was. This is especially true when it comes to short stories, a form that I appreciate most when it involves the literary equivalent of a swift kick in the gut (I am reminded of Joe R. Lansdale, who said of his brilliant story *The Night They Missed the Horror Show* that it was, in his words, a story that didn't blink). I'm all for style, and psychological insight, and that Hemingwayesque "moment of epiphany," but what I really dig are stories that rev it up and go.

For me (and maybe for you), the best kind of short story writers are the ones who keep their sights focused squarely on the story, who understand pacing and action and momentum and that hot little twist at the end. Writers like Ray Bradbury, Richard Matheson, Jack Finney, and Stephen King.

For readers interested in further forays into the world of the short story, I offer humbly a list of some of my own favorites. You could do worse, I think, than the unsettling wonders and dark dreams listed below.

1. Dark They Were, and Golden-Eyed by Ray Bradbury
2. The Monkey's Paw by W.W. Jacobs
3. The Road Virus Heads North by Stephen King
4. The Little Room by Madeline Wynne
5. Dress of White Silk by Richard Matheson
6. Mrs. Spencer and the Oberons by Shirley Jackson
7. The Glass Eye by John Keir Cross
8. The Barnum Museum by Steven Millhauser
9. Tragic Life Stories by Steve Duffy
10. A Rose for Emily by William Faulkner
11. Lucy Has a List by John Sandford
12. 20th Century Ghost by Joe Hill
13. Vampire Lake by Norman Partridge

Until we meet again, fair reader. Long days and pleasant nights.

ABOUT THE AUTHOR

Tyler Miller grew up in Lake Chelan, Washington.
He is the award-winning author of the short story
collection *Stranger Calls: Dark Tales*.
Learn more about Tyler's work at:
www.tylermillerwrites.com.